For Ella, the winter baby

The Winter Wedding

Abby Clements

**SIMON &
SCHUSTER**

London · New York · Sydney · Toronto · New Delhi

A CBS COMPANY

First published in Great Britain by Simon & Schuster UK Ltd, 2015
A CBS COMPANY

3 5 7 9 10 8 6 4

Simon & Schuster UK Ltd
1st Floor
222 Gray's Inn Road
London WC1X 8HB

www.simonandschuster.co.uk

Simon & Schuster Australia, Sydney
Simon & Schuster India, New Delhi

A CIP catalogue record for this book
is available from the British Library

Paperback ISBN: 978-1-47113-701-3
eBook ISBN: 978-1-47113-701-3

Typeset in the UK by M Rules
Printed and bound by CPI Group (UK) Ltd, Croydon, CR0 4YY

The Winter Wedding

Prologue

Our journey started twenty-nine years ago, in Bidcombe, a village nestled in the English countryside, where everyone would come to know our names. Not due to any great virtue or scandal – but simply through the fact that we weren't like the other girls; Lila and I were two halves of a whole. Through the years, we began to separate, but we never really stopped thinking each other's thoughts.

At the start of the nine months, Lila and I shared a space smaller than a rosebud, nestled up against one another within the walls that cradled us. The two of us grew: to the size of a brioche, a stack of freshly baked muffins, then a ballet shoe bag, with us – top to tail – the slippers. For those nine months, our own swirling, kicking limbs, and the blurred sounds of our mum's singing filtering in from outside, were the rhythms of our world. At the moment of the scan – when our parents' hearts must have been racing with the news – one of us was sucking her thumb and the other giving a regal wave. The scan is grainy, you can't see much at all really, but that was Dad's take on it. He said that, even though they knew it was more likely after the treatment, he and Mum were in such deep shock at the news they were having twins that they didn't know what to say. They'd wanted a baby for ten years and now, responding to their call twofold, here were both of us at once.

We were born, squirming and squalling, in our local hospital on a frosty day. I don't remember that bit, of course, but our mum, Alison, and dad, Simon, never tire of telling us about it, showing us photos. They named me, Hazel Delaney, older by ten minutes – and then Lila, my twin sister.

Mum and Dad took us back to their house – a 1920s cottage perched on the outskirts of the village, where they still live. Bidcombe isn't far from London – only an hour and a half on the train – but it's a world away. The kind of place people stop on the streets to talk to you, where the people who work in the bakery, post office, pub and library are your friends. Mum and Dad had lived there as a couple since they were in their early twenties, and now they were returning, joyfully, as an instant family of four. The neighbours had tied balloons to their gates to welcome us.

Mum said everything had been ready for months: our double pram, the matching cots, Winnie-the-Pooh high chairs – in our family photo album we were almost always side by side. Christmases at our cottage were the most special time of year, and there were dozens of photos of those, Mum or Dad smiling and staring at us proudly, their glasses of fizz on the mantelpiece, and the two of us ripping paper off our presents. Our grandmother was there too – Mum's mum, Joyce. It was our Grandma Joyce who first taught me the pleasure of a kitchen full of baking smells – and the joy of a Christmas snowflake cookie still warm, swiped from the cooling rack. Ben arrived when we were four. Mum and Dad were delighted – they hadn't expected to have another child after us, but we must have unwittingly kickstarted something, because he'd come along easily. No matter what else was happening in our lives, Christmas was a time for coming together as a family, the everyday squabbles forgotten as we ate and drank, and played board games, and got on with our new Christmas Day squabbles over toys, and batteries, and the remote.

The cottage was a happy place for us to grow up into children, then to teenagers. Lila and I went to the same primary school, close by. We sat together in class when we could, but at breaktime, Lila would be with the other girls playing French elastic, while I swapped Star Wars stickers with the boys, or showed them my newest comics. There was something irresistibly clandestine about sharing the comics, because they weren't bought with my pocket money, but with secret funds from my dad. Dad was an accountant, still is – trusted by his clients and dedicated to his work. But I knew that deep down he wanted to be a superhero just as much as I did. And that's why, even though it wasn't age-appropriate – or whatever reason it was that Mum used to justify denying me the books and magazines I wanted most – he sometimes helped me buy them.

As teenagers Lila and I stepped apart from one another – Lila spent her spare time in dance classes and I spent mine at the skate park with Sam, my best friend – we'd been joined at the hip since Year 9. Sam was happy to have found someone who loved skateboarding as much as he did – even if I was a girl.

Lila and I stopped looking so alike. I dyed my half of our straight mousey hair a deep dark red, and cut a short fringe, Lila lightened hers with hints of blonde. My curves blossomed and continued to, hers disappeared as soon as they'd arrived.

Our connection remained the same, a network of golden strands, each a memory of a whispered secret or a shared moment that linked us. We weren't bound closely, Lila and me, our togetherness freed us. As we grew from girls to teenagers, she would do her thing, and I'd do mine, but each evening, after dinner, we'd talk in our room until late, giggling together and talking through everything that had taken place that day, or on other days talking about nothing at all.

I don't know if anyone else, outside of our family, really saw how much we relied on one another. But I knew something, deep down – which was that losing Lila would be like losing the air I breathed.

Our A-level results came in, and Lila decided she definitely wanted to study ballet – and we faced the very real prospect that our paths might be diverging. But in the end, when we left home at eighteen, we made sure they didn't. We moved to London together, Lila went to dance school and I studied set design at Central St Martin's college, but we'd come back home to our rented east London flat in the evening, catching up over dinner and wine with friends or – often – just the two of us. Lila went out with friends to dance shows, I'd stay in and watch movies. We were both happy. The flat had been an idea for a long time – as teenagers Lila and I had spent evenings talking about it, fantasising about living in the city in our own place.

Today, I leaned back in my striped deckchair, and looked out across the canal and east London's Victoria Park. I recalled how it had felt, flat-hunting with Lila, wondering if we'd ever find anywhere we could afford, and that we liked enough. Then we heard about this place, a converted warehouse, and decided to have a look. The bedrooms weren't the largest, but the white-painted exposed floorboards brightened up the space, and both of the rooms had large

5

windows. Our living space was cosy, and I say that in estate agent's speak, but that had never mattered to us; we were used to living in each other's space. It was when I had looked out of the window and seen the green space that I'd really fallen in love.

Right now, bikes wove lines through the park, groups of people clustered around picnic blankets and benches, appearing the size of Playmobil figures from my vantage point. The distant sound of reggae playing out tinnily from speakers drifted up to the balcony. The flowers that Lila and I had planted last year were coming back into bloom.

When Lila and I were living together, it might not have always looked like paradise to an outsider – but for us it was. We occasionally argued, sure. Lila would sometimes tidy things away in the kitchen before I'd even used them, and that drove me nuts. As did her constant cushion-plumping while I was watching films. She'd occasionally complain about my singing in the bathroom, or interrupt my midnight baking sessions – emerging from her room, bleary-eyed, asking what on earth I was doing, and couldn't it wait till morning.

On reflection, she'd never really bought in to the idea of Pablo. Lila had, actually, insisted that getting a cat without consulting her was 'completely unreasonable'. But his nibbled ear and bent tail, patches of missing fur, all told the tale of a harrowing life as a street cat that I wasn't able to ignore. I'd had to push that one through.

When winter came and the nights drew in, we'd hole up and spend our evenings on the sofa. Come Christmas, I'd start the baking, and she'd put up our family Advent calendar, filling it with small wooden decorations that we placed on the tree. We'd happily count the days until we went back home to Mum and Dad's.

When we had graduated, in our early twenties, we'd stayed on in the flat. I was doing bar work at the weekends, Lila spending the weekdays auditioning for dance roles, and me scouring the job ads for anything related to set design. Then, well, just anything at all. Unlike Lila, I'd never once lost sleep figuring out the meaning of life, though. Because I knew where it was – there in the silvered memories of the nights we spent together or with our friends, the ones where we laughed so hard our sides hurt.

I was never going to win any prizes for long-term relationships, but I was OK with that. I'd had a few boyfriends, and we'd had fun, but we'd never made it past the six-month mark. Our connections had fizzled out or slipped into friendship. When they'd ended, I'd always felt sort of relieved that I could return to normal life, stop trying to make something work that wasn't really sticking. I guess at the back of my mind there was always Sam – always the question of whether we might stand a chance as more than just friends. And no one else really seemed to match up to him.

And however dates went, I always had Lila and the flat to

come back to. Lila's passion for ballet dancing was as strong as ever, and over the years I'd done what I could to help her keep the faith. She was talented – we both knew that – and she'd had some great parts over the years, but she'd also had a lot of auditions that hadn't led to anything. As she'd waited for her big break, she'd worked as a PA at a city bank during the day, which she did for the money, and at a canalside bar two evenings a week, which she enjoyed more. It was at that bar that she first met Ollie. I was there that night, whiling away the evening over a Pimm's and lemonade.

I'd seen him right away – walking into the bar with a couple of friends, tall and dark, with black-framed glasses, a slightly intense expression and a wonky smile. He was every-thing Lila didn't normally go for – she had a penchant for traditionally handsome, self-involved actors. I was usually the shoulder to cry on at the end of the night. I caught my sister's eye and nodded in Ollie's direction, so that she'd be sure to be the one to take his drinks order.

Before long, the two of them were flirting – and by the end of the night he'd asked for her number. They went on a few dates. Then, gradually, he started appearing with increas-ing frequency at our flat, joining us for mid-week dinners and weekend tea and cake stops. I didn't mind, in fact I liked it – Lila's exes had generally left her wrung-out and tearful, and here was a man who brought out the laughter and lightness in her. It had been at our twenty-seventh birthday party that I realised he was something serious. He'd helped Lila pour drinks, his gaze following my sister around the room with something approaching puppy-dog adoration, even as he pretended to listen to what his friends were saying. And Lila – I saw her looking back once or twice too. I guess that was when I started to realise for the first time that I was going to have to share my sister.

That summer Ollie had become a permanent fixture at our flat, and Lila was happier than I'd ever seen her. She looked so right by his side, his arm draped around her shoulder. Ollie was a lovely guy. And he adored her. There was absolutely nothing wrong with Ollie. Apart from that I knew right away he was The One. The one who would take Lila away from me for good.

At our flat we'd laughed, partied and lounged on the sofa watching films for close to a decade. But now, at twenty-nice – it was only me here. Lila had moved on, and moved out.

This was it – Lila and Hazel, Hazel and Lila had become . . . Lila and Ollie. Everything had started to change.

Chapter 1

Spring sunshine dappled the miniature set I was working on at my desk at home. I squinted against the light and pasted a tiny strip of wallpaper up onto the back wall of the living room – the final piece of the scene in place. A miniature mantelpiece and gilt mirror that I'd found on eBay were positioned just to the side of it, with an intricately embroidered Persian rug the size of a small envelope on the floor below. The room had kept me occupied for weeks now and it was finally finished. It had been something to do, since Lila moved out and in with Ollie.

From my box of figurines, I extracted a man – in a little white shirt, and jeans, his wooden feet protruding from the bottom of the trousers – and his counterpart, a woman in a sweet blue tea dress, her dark brown hair in bunches and a smile fixed in place. I put them next to one another on the sofa, and placed a hardback book I'd made myself – no larger than a postage stamp – in her hands, and a miniscule wine glass in his. They would be talking about their day at work, I imagined, and later they'd retreat upstairs, to the room I'd prepared for them – a bed laid with fresh white linen and a window draped with dark green curtains. The picture frames on the way up the stairs told the story of their lives together. One day I'd find someone to write the story that went with the set. But until that day came, I just liked to look at the little world I'd created and well, I guess enjoy that scrap of control that I felt I had – an imaginary place where everything went according to plan.

I didn't let anyone look at my sets. Not even Sam. In fact – especially not Sam. He'd heard about them once, when we were teenagers, from Lila.

'You're still playing with dolls' houses?' he'd said, laughing. 'I thought you were a tomboy – I mean that's what I liked about you. But I guess you're girlier than I thought.' I'd glared at Lila and wanted the ground to open up and absorb me into it.

Because sharing your dream with someone – letting them have a glimpse of the person you really were – I had a feeling it was supposed to feel different from how that did.

On Monday morning the weekend sun had faded away and left a damp day with a hint of drizzle, the kind that suggests that the spring you glimpsed might never come back. I put on my cycle helmet and rode into work. East London's roads were the same traffic-clogged arteries as always, but I'd learned which backstreets to use to avoid the lorries and the cars, and where you could still, sometimes, hear the birdsong. I never listened to my iPod on the ride, I preferred to focus on what was around me – I don't scare easily, but it seems like a sensible way to, you know, stay alive. Anyway, it was an easy enough decision today as the last time I saw her, I'd picked up Lila's iPod instead of my own, which meant ballet, jazz and classical rather than the music that I usually listened to.

I pulled up outside the Twenty-One offices, in a quiet backstreet in Clerkenwell, and chained my bike up there. I'd been in the job a couple of years now. The TV production company was small but growing fast, producing some of the country's leading costume dramas. The office was always buzzing with the excitement of imminent filming – and I helped out with whatever needed doing in the art department, from sourcing props to making last-minute changes to the sets.

I hadn't got the job right away, despite being twenty-seven. I'd started out two years ago as an intern, and after a couple of months my savings had been down to the final penny. Catching a glimpse of a B-list celebrity, or sharing a joke with some of the staff might have brightened my day but it certainly wasn't paying the bills. I knew I couldn't stay without getting paid. Thankfully the stars aligned and that was when the opening arose for an Art Department Assistant. A junior role – but a job all the same.

OK, so Emma wasn't always the easiest boss to work for – but she had my back. That's what she always said. And day to day, I loved the work, sourcing props, furniture and accessories that would bring each set perfectly to life. I had sort of hoped I'd be promoted by now, but Emma had assured me that a newly created Set Designer role had been earmarked for me. They'd be announcing my promotion any day now, she'd promised. I was kind of relying on it – financially, it was the only way I'd be able to stay on at the flat without replacing Lila.

Josh, the assistant director of some of the company's key shows, braked, coming to a stop next to me.

'Morning,' he said brightly. He took off his helmet and ran a hand roughly over his dark hair, which had gone a little flat. He was wearing a green and blue checked lumberjack shirt over a white t-shirt, light against his olive skin. 'You're in early.'

'Yes. Felt like getting a head start on the day today.'

He locked his bike up next to mine. Josh and I rarely worked together directly, but he often found a reason to stop by my desk for a chat or to drop off a cup of tea, and he was one of the colleagues I got on best with.

'Good weekend?' he asked.

'Not bad,' I said, trying not to think about how lonely the flat had begun to feel. 'How about yours?'

'Good,' he said. 'It was our anniversary – Sarah and I met four years ago yesterday.'

'Congratulations. What did you do to celebrate?'

'Dinner, a film.'

When Josh spoke about his girlfriend, his whole face lit up. It didn't matter whether he was talking about her views on the new exhibition at the Tate Gallery, or the meatballs they'd had at IKEA. She sounded dynamic, fun and carefree, and seemed to charm everyone she met. It was kind of weird, really, that I'd never met her, given that Josh and I had become quite close. But a lot of people choose to keep work and life separate, I reasoned.

'Did she get that new job?'

'At the private gallery?' Josh said. 'Yes. She's got a short contract there. She says she doesn't know where she'll be in the summer.'

'Right,' I said. We went inside the building, and took the steps up to the office at a leisurely pace, both savouring these final few moments before the onslaught of emails and demands started. 'Where are you planning on being this summer? You're not going to jet off somewhere sunny when filming for *Christmas at the Manor* is due to start, are you?'

Our latest project was a popular drama series that ran all year – with one of our most generous budgets for costumes and sets. I'd been longing to work on it, and my boss Emma, while seeming reluctant at first, had finally relented. It would be my first solo project, designing and sourcing props, making the Christmas special really sparkle. She knew she owed me one. I'd covered for a lot of her very long lunches, and these days each morning seemed to begin with a hangover for her, and a coffee shop errand for me. Josh handled the actors, while I would be managing the backdrops, the scenes where he and the cast brought arguments, kisses, and shared intimacies to life.

I liked working with Josh. He was easy to talk things through with, laidback, and had a genuine creative vision that was rare, even in our industry. Plus he made me laugh. Which goes a long way, when it's midnight, and you're both still in the office getting something together for an early start filming.

Josh smiled warmly. 'Don't worry. We're not going anywhere soon. Sarah's desperate to get away, but with our schedule here it'll be a long weekend rather than the long-haul trip she's been dreaming of.'

'Phew. So Sarah wants to do another big trip?'

'Sarah always wants to do a big trip,' he said wearily, but kindly. That was love, I guess – you didn't always have to agree, but you always tried to make each other happy. 'But I'm not going to throw in this job to lie on a beach, however tempting the idea might sometimes be.'

'Well, that's good. For us at least.'

We walked into the office – a large warehouse-style space with more break-out areas and coffee machines than actual desks, and I sat down in my usual spot.

Emma came over to my desk, and leaned over the divider. Her long dark brown curls were loose, and she had bright red lipstick on, which distracted a little from the dark circles under her eyes.

'Hazel, I've got to run to a meeting in a minute, but I just wanted to check you have everything sorted for the shoot on Friday. Did you manage to source the Arts and Crafts chairs we talked about?'

'Yes, that's all sorted,' I said. 'The furniture's due to arrive at the house on Friday, so there'll be time for me to set everything up before we shoot.'

'Great. And the hair stuff?'

'The vintage hair decorations? Yes, I have those here in the office.'

'OK,' Emma said. 'I knew it would be in safe hands with you.'

'Anything else you need?'

'Yes,' she said, pointing to her in-tray. 'That lot. I'm going to square with you, Hazel.' She said it in that conspiratorial way that made it seem as if she was letting me into the fold, that I was privileged really, to be allowed to help her out. I was one of only two people in the office who knew that she was going through a messy divorce.

'I feel like death this morning, and we've got the Americans coming over this afternoon. I'm pretty much obliged to start drinking at lunchtime again today, and that means I'll have to have a massage this morning or I won't be able to face it. It's as simple as that.'

I hesitated. Her divorce was nearly final now, so presumably the end was in sight for this kind of demand.

'This is the last time I ask you to cover for me,' Emma begged, rubbing the skin on her brow. 'I swear, Hazel.'

'OK,' I said, reluctantly. 'I'll do it this last time.'

Everything would be OK once I was promoted – I'd have a salary I could just about live on, and, as importantly, the creative freedom to fulfil my vision for the sets. All I had to do was wait.

Josh and I sat at his desk and worked through the designs for *Christmas at the Manor*. 'I know just the place to get the costumes done,' I said. 'There's a fantastic dressmaker just off Columbia Road.'

'Great.' Josh said, looking over my designs. 'I really like what you've done here with the living room. The chandelier and chaise longue are perfect.'

'Thank you. How are things going with the casting?'

'Good. Mostly. We've got some new talent in for the Christmas episode. Amy Strachan to play one of Edward's sisters.'

'Oh yes – I've heard of her. She was the assistant in the last *Doctor Who*, right? Petite, big eyes?'

'That's her. She's great – I think we've caught her at a really interesting time in her career, and she and Matt have good on-screen chemistry.'

'I look forward to meeting her soon.'

'Come along and watch us film next time. I'll clear it with Emma.'

'That would be great.'

'Hopefully soon I won't have to. It's about time you had a bit more freedom around here.'

'It won't be long, I'm sure.'

Later that day, Lila and I met for lunch in a café on the Regent's Canal. It was a sunny morning in March, and joggers and dog-walkers passed us by on the towpath. I'd got her text first thing in the morning:

Big news, Sis. Lunch? Lx

Lila was holding out her hand toward me, a red and yellow Haribo ring on the fourth finger. Her hooded green eyes – mine, genes courtesy of our mum – danced with excitement, a trace of bronze shadow on the lids. 'This is just a stand-in, obviously,' she said, a smile playing on her lips. 'He's going to pick out a real one.'

Woah. This was really happening. My sister was engaged. 'Congratulations!' I hugged her.

It made sense. She and Ollie had been living together for four months now, and everything seemed to have worked out well. They were as compatible as hot chocolate and marshmallows, raisins and scones, red velvet cupcakes and vanilla icing . . . you get the picture. Ollie was starry-eyed over my sister, and it had been clear for a while that things were heading in a particular direction. With church bells.

But it still hit me hard. Lila was getting married. Lila, my little sister, if only by a few minutes, was going to walk down the aisle with Ollie. I was happy for her. And yet – God, this is kind of embarrassing to admit – I was a bit jealous.

It wasn't that I wanted to be in her position – getting married had always appealed more to her than me. And like I said, I don't mind Ollie. I actually kind of like him. But I guess I realised that perhaps the reason I hadn't quite been able to face filling the spare room with someone new, even though it was breaking me financially, was because I'd wondered if there was the chance she might, one day, come back.

And now? There was no way that would be happening.

Where would I be without Lila? I mean *really* without Lila? This was permanent.

The other side of her coin was Ollie, now. Who am I kidding, it had been for a while now. But the other side of mine ... Can a coin even exist if it doesn't have another side?

Oblivious, Lila started to tell me the story.

'We went to Cabana, you know the rooftop bar over-looking Covent Garden, and he'd got us a table in the corner, really quiet and candlelit. We had dinner there, and we were talking about this and that, nothing important – an audition I did yesterday – and then he asked me.'

'Was it a surprise?'

'Mostly. I mean we'd talked about marriage – but I didn't see the proposal coming, not when it did.'

'He did well, then. And you seem happy.'

'I am,' she said. And it showed, it had done ever since she met Ollie – in the brightness of her green eyes, the sway in her step, everything that a string of rejections from dance companies and shows had almost knocked out of her. 'I think when you know, you know, don't you?'

'That's great.' I hugged her again. 'And I know what you mean. There's something about you and Ollie – you just *fit*. Have you talked about when?'

'I don't know ... we didn't talk about dates, but neither of us wants to wait long.' She paused and looked at me. 'I've heard about a great wedding planner – Suzanne. A couple of friends have used her. Reasonable rates and apparently she makes the whole thing completely stress-free.'

'Sounds ideal,' I said. 'You sure you can afford it, though?'

'Yes. I've been putting a little aside for a while. Ollie has too. I guess we were both considering this as a possibility, and we want to do it properly.'

'Have you told Mum and Dad yet?'

'Not yet,' she said, with an excited smile. 'I want to do it in person. Care to join us this weekend?'

'Back to Bidcombe?'

Lila nodded.

'Sure. That would be fun. Will Ben be there?'

'I hope so. I've called him, left a couple of messages. So hopefully he'll be able to make it.'

Leaving our brother messages hadn't got me very far over the past couple of months, but I didn't want to dampen Lila's enthusiasm.

'Hazel. Changing the subject I know, but do you think we should talk about . . .'

'The flat?' I said. I knew this was coming. But I just wasn't quite ready to face the idea of living in our flat with anyone but my twin sister. 'It'll work itself out . . .'

I tried not to think of the pile of unpaid bills by the door.

Lila's expression softened. 'It's been four months, Haze. It's not going to work itself out.'

I couldn't go on living in a two-bedroom flat much longer, I knew that. It was crazy. One more month was all I had before I had to go to my parents to borrow money – and

I really didn't want to do that. But the idea of living with someone other than Lila was still weird for me.

'I'll look around. And who knows, hopefully when I get this promotion, I won't need anyone else for the second room. I might even be able to pay for the flat myself.'

'OK, OK,' Lila said, apologetically. 'It's your business. Sorry. I shouldn't have mentioned it.'

I sipped my drink. If I really had to, I'd start looking. But I was confident it wouldn't come to that.

Chapter 2

The next day at work, the CEO of Twenty-One, Aaron, waved us all into the boardroom first thing in the morning. 'Quick meeting, guys – come on in. And don't look so worried, it's good news.'

I walked with the others, joining the rest of the company in the steel and glass meeting room.

'Morning everyone, grab yourselves some coffee,' Aaron said more brightly, once everyone – about thirty of us – was in there. Was this it? Would this be the morning he announced my promotion?

'As you all know, Twenty-One is entering an exciting period of growth, and I've brought you all here this morning to talk about the creation of two new positions.'

A flush of excitement came to my cheeks. So, today was the day. I looked around for Emma, and could just make her out at the back of the crowd. I turned back.

Aaron caught my eye, and I smiled. He then looked to

his right. 'I'm delighted to introduce you to Tim Graham.'

Tim was in his mid-thirties, with a hipster beard and short-sleeved shirt rolled up to his shoulders and an anchor tattoo just visible underneath.

Who was this guy? My chest grew tight.

'Tim's going to be our newest Set Designer.'

The punch of his words hit me in the stomach. Then, a wave of disbelief. Emma had promised me – she'd been certain, she'd said all along that they'd recruit internally.

Perhaps I was jumping the gun. Aaron had said two jobs, hadn't he?

'Tim joins us from Hetrodox TV with his assistant, Amber McGuire.'

My gaze went to the woman at Tim's side. Amber was about my age, maybe a year or two older, with glossy dyed black hair and tortoiseshell glasses. She was wearing a vintage jade blouse with cocktail glasses on it and flared skirt.

So we'd both be assistants. Working in parallel. So, in the unlikely event that a new position opened up again, I guess she'd now also be in the running. I felt the future I'd envisioned slip away. The salary I'd thought I'd be on, that would enable me to keep living on my own, now seemed out of reach.

'Should take some of the heat off you, Hazel,' Aaron said cheerfully. 'We all know how busy you are.'

I nodded, feeling numb. I didn't want to speak in case the tears that were prickling at my eyes spilled over.

'And what's more,' Aaron said, jubilantly, 'Amber's brought us cakes! She must have heard a rumour about what we run on round here.'

Shyly, Amber brought forth a plate of iced cupcakes, decorated with silver balls. The cakes were perfect. Absolutely perfect.

'Pssst. Haze, come in for a chat?' Emma said, beckoning me into her office as I passed.

I ducked inside and closed the door behind me.

'Bloody hell. Well, this is awkward,' she said, shaking her head. 'So sorry about that. I had no idea they'd look outside the company.'

I felt shell-shocked from the news, and tears welled in my eyes.

'For some weird reason they left me out of the decision,' Emma said, frowning, 'which obviously I'm not at all happy about.'

'Right,' I said, willing the tears not to fall. 'Well, you weren't to know then. I'm sure something else will come up.'

'That's the spirit,' Emma said, hurriedly. 'Anyway, I'm sure that hipster dude, whatever his name is . . .'

'Tim,' I said.

'I bet Tim won't last five minutes,' Emma said. 'You'll get your promotion, Haze. I'm sure of it.'

*

Back at the flat, I poured myself a glass of red wine. I still felt dazed by Aaron's announcement. The new reality was starting to sink in and I wanted to talk to someone. I glanced over at Lila's empty room. She and Ollie would probably be out celebrating tonight.

I thought through my other options – Sam. We'd barely spoken since Christmas. I longed to hear his voice now, but I couldn't call him. I didn't want him to hear me like this.

I don't like to have regrets, but I guess I did regret this one thing. We'd been at a Christmas party, hosted by Edie and Joe, schoolfriends of mine and Sam's. A few glasses of mulled wine down, I'd got the idea into my head that now was the time. I'd had feelings for Sam for years. I'd needed to know if he felt the same way. I'd moved a little closer to him on the sofa, as we talked.

He'd looked into my eyes and in that split-second I'd seen our lives coming together in a new way. It had made my heart leap, and the moment felt full of potential.

Then I'd leaned in towards him and Sam's face had paled.

'I'm sorry,' he'd said, mumbling and pushing his hair away from his face. 'Haze. I didn't . . . This is weird.' He had practically rushed out of the room, turning his back on the party. Through the living room window I'd watched him walking away down the snow-covered street, snowflakes settling in his hair, and I'd felt sick to my stomach at what I'd done.

Since then we hadn't talked, save the occasional text. He

told me he was back in Bidcombe, living with his parents again. He'd got a job as a P.E. teacher at our old school. We still hadn't discussed what had happened.

It wasn't the rejection that hurt most. It was feeling like I'd lost my best friend. I missed Sam, badly. Remembering that night, and the stupid mistake I'd made, I drank slowly, until, fuzzy-headed, I fell asleep.

That weekend, Lila, Ollie and I took a train back to Bidcombe, and then walked from the station to the cottage. I tried not to think about Sam. That wasn't why we were here. I was relieved when we passed his street, and moved on towards the one we'd grown up on.

Mum greeted us at the cottage door, with a smile and hug. 'Come in, come in,' she said. She squeezed Ollie's hands. 'It's great to see you again, Ollie. It's been a while since you came up this way, hasn't it?'

She ushered us in, and started pouring us all mugs of tea and putting some Hobnobs on a plate.

I'm making her sound like the perfect mother and house-wife, aren't I? The biscuits, the warm welcome. I love my mum, and she's always been there for me. But if I left it at that – well, it wouldn't be giving the full picture.

Our mum, Alison, is the kind of woman who stands out in a village like Bidcombe. It's not just her unruly brown hair, or her clothes – charity-shop finds mixed with jeans and

Indian headscarves. It's more the way she's never thought twice about telling it how it is, or hesitated for a moment considering what someone would think of her.

Sometimes I've wondered why she had ever chosen the cottage, this place – but she always said that having grown up in a city herself she wanted something different – for herself, and then for us. Her job, as a counsellor, was based in the nearest town, a half-hour's drive away. She had a treatment room there, working mainly with young people. Before she'd had me and Lila, she'd been a journalist at the same tabloid Dad had once done accounts for, but, her edges softened a little by having children (she said), she never went back to Fleet Street. Dad set up his own firm in the village, and she retrained, starting up work properly when Ben was in school. I hadn't appreciated it at the time, but now I saw that her time on the school run had never been easy. While the other mothers chatted easily together, I think our mum always felt a bit like an outsider.

Mum would often be thinking about the case she was working on, and she'd forget to say the right thing to the right person about their new Yorkshire terrier or planned kitchen extension. She rarely got round to making things for the village bake sale. But she loved us, always had. The people she was close to she looked after with endless loyalty.

Dad was in our living room, and jumped quickly to his feet when we came in. He hugged Lila, then me. It always made me feel complete, hugging Dad. The man who'd responded to our cries at night, cooked us fish fingers and alphabetti spaghetti, allayed our fears of spiders, bullies, then, as we took tentative steps into our twenties, professional failure. He looked smaller, somehow, since we'd all left home. His life and Mum's – once big and sprawling and loud with the three of us – must be much quieter now.

'Well we did rather hope Ben would be able to make it,' Mum said apologetically. 'When you said it was important, I asked if he'd come back too, but he said he was too busy.'

I turned to Lila. 'I already guessed as much,' she said, with an air of resignation. 'When he didn't call me back I assumed that was the case.'

'It doesn't matter,' Ollie said, matter-of-factly. 'We can fill Ben in later.'

So, I should tell you about Ben. My flesh and blood, just like Lila. The family resemblance is hard to miss – he looks very much like a younger version of Dad, tall and well-proportioned, with a defined dark brow and a nose with a slight bend in it, something Lila and I missed when the genes were being handed out. When I answer the phone, it's hard to tell the difference between Dad and Ben, so similar are their voices. Dad exudes warmth and inspires confidence – and Ben has that same quality too. Or at least, he used to have it.

Ben and I used to chat and laugh and play endlessly in the park as kids. But he didn't seem to have much time for me

and Lila these days. He'd been distant for a while, since starting a new job in banking. I hoped that soon things would get
back to normal, and we'd laugh about old times again, share
jokes around the dinner table, remember the wildness of the
summers spent in our garden. More than anything, I hoped
that at Lila's wedding, and at Christmas, we could be a
normal family.

Mum brought her brown curls up into a loose bun, and
secured it with a hairband. 'Sorry, I'm a bit all over the place
today,' she said.

It was nothing new, or out of the ordinary, but Mum
would say things like that when we visited to give the
impression that it was. That her usual life was slick, and well
organised.

'I had a call from a client this morning, and well … it's
kind of thrown me, I suppose. I wanted so much to help
him, but I feel like I'm running out of time. He's been in the
system since he was six … petty crime, then leading on to
this …' she glanced up at me, and the strain was evident in
her green eyes.

'I've got a file this thick on him,' Mum said, 'and I've been
alerting social services for months now …'

'Alison,' Dad said, gently.

'It only happened this morning, Simon. These are people
who …'

'I know it's important,' Dad said, his voice measured and

calm. 'But I get the sense that Lila and Ollie have come here for a reason today. Don't you?'

'Sorry,' Mum said, her cheeks colouring. 'Oh God, I was rambling on, wasn't I? And after all of you have come all this way. I'm not normally like this, you know that . . .' She took a breath and seemed to compose herself. 'Go on, Lila.' She smiled broadly. That warm, wide smile. She's beautiful, Mum. She had a way of drawing people to her. Our friends always said they felt that they could tell her anything, she made them want to open up and confess everything bad they'd ever done, and, with the forgiveness in that smile, it would be OK.

Lila took Ollie's hand in hers and brought it into her lap.

'I knew it,' Dad said. Tears sprung to his eyes. 'You're getting married.'

'Oh don't, Simon,' Mum said, laughing. 'It's not the same these days, this generation. Let them enjoy being young and happy, just because we rushed in doesn't mean . . .'

The shine in Lila's eyes as she got ready to present her and Ollie's news, was starting to fade. I saw Ollie squeeze her hand gently, urging her on.

Lila coughed. 'Well Dad's right actually. We *are* getting married.' She beamed.

Mum, blushing furiously now, hugged them both. 'Well – aren't I the fool. That's fantastic.'

'Thanks,' Lila said. Ollie looked as if he might burst with pride as he shook Dad's hand.

'I'm so happy for you,' Dad said, hugging Ollie in a heart-felt burst of affection. 'Brilliant news.'

Mum looked a little dazed at first, but then smiled. 'Lovely news, isn't it?' she said to Dad.

'Have you set a date yet?' Dad asked.

'August,' Ollie said. 'We know it's soon, but we both want a summer wedding and we don't want to wait until next year. I'm not sure we could, really,' he said, smiling at my sister.

'I've found a fantastic wedding planner. Suzanne. And I have a bit of time on my hands at the moment too.'

Lila's dance career had hit a wall this past year, as she'd had only a scattering of parts. She talked, often, about her age and when she should retire. But there were some ballerinas who kept going into their late thirties or even forties, I told her. She was still fit. And she still had her dreams.

'A summer wedding, lovely,' Mum said. Her eyes grew a little shiny as she took Lila by the hand. 'My little girl.' She smiled. 'You're all grown up.'

'I already was,' Lila said, laughing it off. 'Getting married won't make any difference.'

But I knew what Mum was thinking. We were all going to have to let Lila go now, and trust that she was in safe hands.

Later that afternoon, Dad came into the kitchen to help me make tea.

'So, what exciting news, eh?' he said, still beaming.

'Yes, great,' I said.

'But we've hardly talked about you,' Dad said. 'How is everything at work? Have they given you that promotion you deserve yet?'

'Nope,' I said, a wave of disappointment flooding back. I took a breath. 'Actually they gave the job to someone else in the end. I think they wanted someone with more experience.'

'Oh no,' Dad said. 'But that doesn't make any sense – you've been working there for ages ... and your boss was always saying ...'

'She says a lot of things,' I said. It was starting to dawn on me that perhaps Emma would always come first for Emma – that she didn't even have it in her to have my best interests at heart. 'I shouldn't have got my hopes up really, not until it was more certain.'

'I'm sorry to hear that. You OK for money? I'm sure me and your mum ...'

'I'm fine,' I lied. I'd been half-wondering all day whether to ask Mum and Dad for the money I needed to tide me over, but it seemed a crass thing to do on Lila and Ollie's day, plus my pride kept niggling at me.

'I mean, I will be,' I corrected myself, 'just as soon as I get someone in for the room in the flat. How hard can it be to find a new Lila?' I laughed, but it came out sounding a little hollow.

'OK,' Dad said, nodding. 'Well, you know we can always help you, if you need something to tide you over.'

I thought of how good it would feel to clear my debts. But I knew this wasn't the right way – I had to sort things out for myself.

We left the cottage for the train station, walking back through the streets of Bidcombe. It had been nice to spend the day with Mum and Dad and to celebrate Lila's good news together as a family. Well, with almost all the family.

'Hey, isn't that . . .?' Lila said, pointing towards the bakery. I looked over, and there he was, chatting to the owner, visible through the glass. His sandy blonde hair and that contagious smile – I could already see it reflected in the expression of the woman serving him. Sam.

I paused outside the door, and butterfly wings fluttered against the walls of my stomach.

Part of me yearned to talk to him, another still burned with the humiliation of the way our last meeting turned out.

Lila went to call out to him, but I put a hand on her arm. 'We haven't got long before the train,' I said. 'Let's just go.'

Lila and Ollie went to the buffet car on the train, leaving me with too much time to think.

I wondered what Sam was doing right now. Sitting in his room, listening to music . . . reading comics. Like the two of us used to do together. Back then I'd see his eyes flicker over the images and it was almost as if I was taking in the story too – I knew I didn't have to wait long until he'd finish, and we'd talk about it together. Sometimes Sam only had to say the first word of a sentence and I'd be able to finish it for him. The detail of his bedroom, the Blu-tacked posters, the worn blue carpet with trains on it. It was strange to walk right past that house now and not stop by. Then it hit me – fifteen years had passed since those days. And while we'd remained friends, a lot of water had passed under the bridge since then.

I saw Lila and Ollie coming back down the aisle of the train, and shrugged off the memory. From the smile on Lila's face, I knew she had something important to say to me.

'I've got a favour to ask,' she said, sitting down.

'Sure. Fire away.'

'Will you be my chief bridesmaid, Hazel?'

I felt tears well in my eyes.

'Say you will?' she prompted me.

I brushed away a tear and smiled, then gave her a big hug. 'Of course I will, silly.'

Chapter 3

The night I got back from the cottage, I placed an ad on Gumtree for a new flatmate. Lila telling our parents about the engagement, and inviting me to be part of the day, had made it all seem more real. Lila was right – I needed to move on – and my bank balance spoke for itself.

Over the course of the week there had been people interested – plenty of them.

It was a Sunday afternoon, and the woman on my sofa, who'd introduced herself as Zuzy ('Two z's'), and was in her early twenties, curled her sock-clad feet up under her. The Kermit faces on them were still peeking out. She cradled her tea in towards her chest, and a smile spread across her face, her cheeks flushed with excitement.

'I'm SO glad I found this place, Hazel. I mean I know the room's not massive, but I don't have much. I had to leave my last flatshare in a bit of a hurry, you see. I left some things behind and I haven't wanted to go back to pick them up. But we weren't *friends* there. That was always the problem.'

I listened to Zuzy, hoping that a natural break in her conversation would come soon. She'd been talking without pausing to draw breath for what felt like at least an hour.

'It's going to be different here – I just know it,' she said, happily. 'Because we are going to be friends, and do everything together.'

At this she let out a small squeal of excitement. Oh God, this felt like it was spiralling out of my control, and I had to claw something back. I coughed loudly and got to my feet. 'So. Thanks so much for coming. It was good to meet you.'

I was a horrible person. I was going to crush this girl's dreams.

'You too,' she said, putting her tea down, looking slightly confused. 'You said the 5th of April, as a move-in date, didn't you?'

'As the potential date, yes,' I said, wishing I'd never said anything about it. 'Anyway, thanks for coming, and I'll let you know what I decide.'

It was awkward, ushering her almost physically out of the front door, but as I closed it I felt an overwhelming rush of relief. It was my choice – I didn't have to give just anyone the keys. And I definitely, definitely wasn't giving them to Zuzy.

The afternoon of interviews had left me with a sinking feeling. The male dental student had talked non-stop about cavity prevention, Zuzy in all her neediness, and then there was the teenage trust-fund girl who'd arrived with a list of interview questions for me. None of them were right. They weren't even close. And I wasn't even being *that* picky.

I thought of the happy times Lila and I had spent at the flat and reminded myself that they were over now. I had to move on – and if that meant compromising, so be it.

Back at the office on Monday, I pinned the advert to the noticeboard by the kettle:

Wanted: flatmate for a spacious
two-bedroomed flat in Bethnal Green.
Must like cakes. And cats.
Contact Hazel@tvtwenty-one.com.

I hadn't planned on asking people at work, but after seeing what the wider world had to offer, I reasoned that at least the people I worked with were relatively sane.

I worked that morning on some minutes for our Monday catch-up meeting, and just before lunchtime a message pinged into my inbox.

To: Hazel Delaney
From: Amber McGuire
Subject: Your ad

Right. For the purposes of identification, I'm the new girl.

I sit over by the photocopier, black hair, glasses. I'm Tim's assistant and sit on my own at lunchtime. That's just the deal of the new girl, I think, as I'm actually OK. Pay rent on time, offer fairly decent company. Have a great selection of box sets.

I'd love to see your flat. When's good for you?

Amber

I glanced around and Amber caught my eye and smiled. Amber – with her long, black hair and tortoiseshell glasses, seemed to have fitted into the office right away. I had been meaning to introduce myself to her properly – I really had. Well, I say meaning to – in that, 'once I've finished this, I'll go right over and say hi' way. I guess I'd been putting it off. Because it would mean seeing her boss Tim, the man who was doing the job I'd hoped I would be doing by now.

But that was hardly Amber's fault. I couldn't just ignore Amber's nice, friendly email – even though part of me longed to do just that. I took a deep breath, swallowed down my pride and walked over to her desk.

'Hi,' I said, 'I'm Hazel. I thought I'd come round in

person. Nice to properly meet you.' I wondered for a moment if I should hold out my hand for her to shake. No, too formal.

'Hey,' she said, seeming so much more laidback than me. 'So your place sounds great, that's just the area I've been looking in. Well – I should say it's the area I started looking in. Since then I've covered pretty much everywhere in zones 1–5. And I haven't ruled out 6 either. The way things have been going I might end up in Manchester.'

She laughed, but looked weary. I remembered how it was when Lila and I had been looking for somewhere, consoling ourselves with wine after seeing yet another dump.

'You should come around.' I did my best to summon up enthusiasm – she did seem nice, she really did – but my voice came out sounding flat. She wasn't Lila. Whichever way I looked at it, she was not my twin sister and never would be.

Her face brightened, and she seemed oblivious to my mixed feelings. 'How about Thursday, after work?'

The day quietened down after that. Emma went home at eleven, which even given her record was pretty early. I took the opportunity to focus on what Lila and I had talked about. One of my first responsibilities was helping with invites, so I got to work designing some mock-ups for invites for Lila and Ollie. At my desk, the dividers giving me a bit of privacy, I played around with fonts on my computer, preparing the designs so that I could print them out on card. I was meeting Lila for lunch, but I wanted to get them just right before I showed her anything.

'Party invites on work time?' I leapt in guilty surprise, and looked up on hearing the male voice. Josh was standing there with a smile on his lips.

'Christ, you made me jump,' I said.

'Sorry, didn't mean to. So what is it? I like that font,' he said pointing to one in an Art Nouveau style.

'They're for my sister's wedding.'

'Nice,' he said. 'When's the wedding?'

'This summer. They want to do it soon.'

'Makes sense,' he said. 'Anyway. When you do get a minute – I'd like to pin down what the Christmas dinner scene is going to look like.'

'This is where it all goes horribly wrong, right?'

'Yes,' he nodded. 'Marianne finds out about the affair, and there's a showdown ... Do you think you could do your thing, Hazel? Source something stylish, historically accurate and extremely reasonable?'

'It would be my pleasure,' I said, making a note on my To-do list.

He lowered his voice, so that only I could hear him.

'You should have got that set designer job, you know. They made a mistake, recruiting externally. You've got way more experience than that Tim guy anyway.'

'Thank you,' I said quietly. 'I appreciate you saying that.'

'It seemed really weird, Emma not putting you forward.'

'She didn't have the chance,' I said. 'They didn't invite her to be part of the discussion ... I guess maybe it's something to do with the way she's been at work lately ...'

Josh looked at me, puzzled.

'That's what she told you?' he said.

My breath caught. What was he talking about?

I nodded, mutely.

'Haze. Look, I don't want to stir. That's the last thing I want to do. But I was at that meeting. Aaron asked about you – he knows as well as we all do how talented you are, how ready you are for a step up. But Emma said you'd been struggling with the workload lately and you'd told her you didn't feel ready.'

His words hung in the air.

'That can't be right,' I said, hoarsely. 'She promised ...' It came out sounding pathetic, and I realised that was exactly what my blind trust in Emma had been.

'You deserved the job,' Josh said. 'We all knew that.'

I went to meet Lila at a cafe on Exmouth Market, a cobbled backstreet lined with cafés and boutiques. She made a beeline for the table where I was sitting, taking her large Mexican-print bag from her shoulder, kissing me hello and sitting down.

'How are things?' she asked brightly.

'Good,' I lied. I didn't feel like going into the ins and outs of what was happening at work, and what Josh had said just now. My head was still spinning with it all. 'The new girl at work – Amber – is coming to see the flat later this week.'

'Great,' Lila said. I could see from her face that she was excited that I had finally kicked off the flatmate-hunt.

'I hope so. She can't be any worse than the people who've already been.'

'That bad?'

'Much worse,' I said, laughing. The procession of nutters looking at her old room seemed funny, now that I was with Lila. Things always did. I knew a lot would remain the same – we'd still talk on the phone, meet up, go to the cinema together. But if Lila woke at 2 a.m. worried about something it would be Ollie she'd turn to – and if she had a dance routine to practise in the kitchen, he'd be the one watching and encouraging her. And I was still getting my head around all of that.

'I'm not sure she's at all right . . .' I realised that the idea of actually liking Amber was scaring me more than the prospect of imminent bankruptcy.

'Give her a chance,' Lila said kindly, sensing my mixed feelings.

I nodded. Lila was right. She was almost always right.

'I'll let you know how I get on.'

'In the meantime, I've had the most amazing morning.'

'What's happened?' I said, leaning in.

'You know that ballet at Sadler's Wells theatre I auditioned for last week?'

'Yes.' I held my breath. It had been a while since we'd had good news.

My sister's face broke into a wide smile, her eyes sparkling and I saw right away that this was big.

Her voice went up a little as she told me the news. 'I got a call and they want me in the show.'

I leapt out of my chair and gave her a warm hug. My arms went right the way round her and even through her jumper I could feel the ridges on her body that mine didn't have. I didn't like the way they felt. I never had. I didn't like feeling that I might crush her.

'That's fantastic,' I said, pulling away to look at her.

'Isn't it? They had someone drop out, and they're starting up in a month, so the schedule is really intense. There'll be rehearsals this spring and a run through the summer.'

'Brilliant. You deserve it. You really do.'

'Thank you. Ollie's really happy about it too. It's just the stepping stone I've needed,' Lila said. 'I've even heard rumours that they're looking out for dancers to take through to *The Nutcracker*, come Christmas time.'

I sucked in my breath. 'Oh my God.'

'Yes. That's my biggest dream, as you know.'

'You could be Clara.'

'I could never be Clara,' she said, shaking her head and smiling. 'Anyway, back down to earth. Ollie's popped to the farmer's market to get us some ingredients for a celebratory meal tonight. That's enough for me.'

'Lovely,' I said.

As Lila lifted her mug of hot chocolate to her lips, her engagement ring caught my eye. Vintage gold with a modest sapphire cradled by tiny diamonds, a perfect cluster of sparkle.

'But this summer?' I said, thinking back over what she'd just said. 'What about the wedding?'

'Oh, it's fine. Suzanne says she's got it all in hand. Employing her was the best thing I could have done.'

Amber came around to the flat on Thursday evening. She swept Pablo up into her arms effortlessly, and stroked him gently along his back. 'What's this one's name?'

'Pablo,' I said. 'He's a rescue.'

'What happened to his ear?' Amber said, touching the missing bit gently.

'He had a rough past. They told me at the shelter that he's tough as nails, but all I've seen is that he's a total softie.'

'He seems to have a lot of character,' Amber said. Pablo purred contentedly in her arms. Something he did very rarely with people he didn't know.

'Come and see the balcony,' I said, opening up the French

doors. From here we could see out over Victoria Park, the streaky sunset backing the silhouetted city.

'This view is what sold the place to me,' I said.

'I can see why,' Amber said, smiling. I took a seat on one of the deckchairs and motioned for her to sit next to me.

'So what do you like to do? When you're not chained to the desk at Twenty-One I mean.'

'Watch films. Late-night baking. Swing dancing. Yep, I think that pretty much covers it,' she said with a smile. 'Oh, and brunch on the weekend after payday, followed by a mooch around a vintage market.'

'Sounds good.'

'You?'

'Quite similar actually. I'm into films too, and get to the cinema when I can. Lila – she's my twin sister, she used to have the room that's free now – she was never very interested, so I kind of got used to going on my own. Is that weird?'

'Not at all,' Amber said. 'Unless I'm a weirdo too. And you bake? I noticed some things in the kitchen.'

'Yes. Though I haven't done that much recently.'

'It'll come back,' she reassured me. 'Was it something you and your sister did together?'

I shook my head. 'Lila's never been into it. She's a dancer, and rehearsals take up most of her time. We were often in and out of the flat at different times, but when our paths crossed – well, it was fun. Having her here.'

'It must've been. Why did she go?'

'She found Mr Right.'

'The flat's good luck in that department then?'

'I can't vouch for that,' I laughed. 'If there were any guarantees I'd be asking for far more rent.'

'Oh don't do that!' Amber said. 'I've accepted that my love life is well and truly over. But it would be amazing to be able to live here, and it's one of the only places I've seen that I can afford.'

I smiled at her eagerness, and the way that without seeming needy, she wasn't playing games. I thought of the relief I'd feel, being able to pay the bills that were mounting up. But then, another feeling that surprised me. It might actually be, well, quite nice to live with Amber. Not living-with-Lila-nice. But new, and fresh, and fun. I knew now what to do.

'How would you feel about coming to live here?' I asked her.

She beamed. 'I think you've just made my day.'

Chapter 4

When Amber agreed to move in, I felt as if a weight had been lifted. I went into work feeling stronger, and determined to have it out with Emma.

'Morning, Haze,' Emma said, brightly.

She was acting as if nothing at all had happened. As if she hadn't lied to me and let me believe she'd look after me, when in fact she'd done the exact opposite.

'You OK?' she said. 'You look a bit out of it this morning.'

I felt my strength desert me in the face of her kind enquiry.

'I'm fine,' I said, wanting to kick myself for my cowardice.

'Great,' she said. 'Because there's a lot to do today and I'm really going to need you to help me with it.'

'Yes?' I said.

'Starting with a Danish pastry, and a coffee. Be a love, would you?'

*

When I returned to the empty flat in the evening, I felt deflated. I'd been so sure I would have the guts to confront Emma, yet I'd utterly failed to. How was I ever going to get anywhere in my career if I let people like her walk all over me?

I started making dinner, feeling down, when I got a call from Lila.

'Tell me you've got half an hour,' she said. 'It's sort of an emergency.'

Lila was round by eight. 'The wedding's going to be a mess, Hazel.'

'Why? What do you mean?'

Her eyes were wide with panic.

'Look, calm down. Deep breaths. Take a seat and tell me what's going on.'

'She's cancelled, Haze. The wedding planner's totally bailed on us.' Tears glistened in her eyes. 'She said she'd taken on too much work.'

Oh God. The last thing that Lila and Ollie needed now was this.

'Could you postpone it?'

'I guess we could,' she said, biting her lip. 'And I haven't ruled it out completely. But I've talked about it with Ollie, and neither of us wants to. We really had our hearts set on getting married this summer. But we need help – these rehearsals are really demanding – and Ollie's just had a commission for a new screenplay that has him up all hours.'

'Mum?' I said. The twitch at the side of her mouth gave away her understandable reservations.

'Perhaps not.'

'Grandma?'

I pictured the colourful pompoms Grandma Joyce was fond of knitting, and could tell Lila was thinking the same thing. We shook our heads in unison.

I didn't want to just plough in there. But then I didn't want to miss my chance, either.

'I'm not that busy at the moment,' I said, hesitantly. It wasn't completely true – but I was determined not to let Emma's demands take over any more of my life. 'And I've already been doing a few things as your chief bridesmaid. Why don't I do it?'

'Would you? You'd do that for me?' Lila said, her eyes wide.

'Of course.'

'Thank you.' She beamed. 'Yes please!'

I felt a bubble of excitement at the task ahead. 'How involved would you like me to be?'

'Do it all,' Lila said, her eyes alight with excitement. 'I trust you completely. But you wouldn't be working from scratch, obviously. I've got something for you,' Lila said, bringing a small embroidered notebook on to her lap. She hesitated for a moment before passing it over to me.

'It's not like I've been planning my wedding for years or anything,' she said, suddenly sheepish.

Her expression told me how treasured the possession was, and I opened it carefully. Inside each page was covered with sketches and ideas, collages of magazines and photos with notes next to them.

'You sure?' I said, laughing.

'Just since I met Ollie. But you can't tell him that,' Lila said, smiling.

I took a closer look at some of the notes and ideas, and was pleased to see that they chimed with the initial concept I'd imagined for the wedding. 'Well, this rather puts the brakes on the Little Mermaid-themed wedding I had planned for you. You know how you used to love that film . . .'

Lila's eyes widened.

I held my hands up. 'I'm joking,' I said. 'Honestly, do you really think I'd do that to you? If we're going to do this together, you need to have a bit more faith in me.'

She smiled, evidently relieved. 'Sorry . . . I do trust you. Really I do. And I'm much happier with you doing this than a total stranger. I wish we'd done this from the very beginning.'

'You only had to ask.' I tucked the book away in my bag. 'Anything else I should know about?'

Lila bit her lip, pondering the question. 'Nope. I think that's it.'

'Then we're all set,' I said. 'I can't wait to start planning for you.'

That weekend, Amber moved into the flat. I helped her carry her boxes of things up the stairs. We were on our second run, and she had piled two on top of each other, so that only a glimpse of her eyes and the top of her head showed above them as she walked. Pablo wove his way around her legs and purred, then scooted off ahead, into her room.

Once inside, I put her things down on the bare floor-boards of what used to be Lila's bedroom. It was simple, but full of light, and had a view of lively urban sprawl where mine looked out onto the park.

'Shall we go back for the rest?' I asked. Her friend had dropped her off, and presumably was still waiting downstairs in the street.

Amber gave a smile and shook her head. 'That's me. That's everything.'

I cast my eye over the half-dozen boxes and couple of bags we'd brought up.

'Really?' This couldn't be everything. I had about four times this amount of stuff – most of which I could probably do without, admittedly – squirrelled away in my room.

'Yes,' she said, unfazed, opening one box. 'And most of it's for the kitchen.' She held a cherry-shaped biscuit cutter in one hand, and a tiny sieve for icing sugar in the other. 'There were some things that had to come, of course.'

She dusted her hands off on her jeans and perched on the edge of the bed, testing it. 'I feel quite settled already.'

'Great,' I said. It suited her, this room. The simplicity of it, the generous casement windows that let the sunshine fall in wide, pale trapezoids on the floor.

'I know what you're thinking,' she said, a sparkle of mischief in her eyes. 'Why doesn't this woman have any stuff?'

I shrugged, but couldn't tell her it wasn't true.

'Messy break-up,' she said. 'Three months ago. Jude. Musician and not-quite-a-grown-up. When we moved in together, I brought almost everything. He'd been living in a houseboat, so he didn't have much – and when I moved out, I left most of my things there.'

'You couldn't bring it with you?'

'Oh, of course I could have – I just didn't really want to. I'm aware it sounds nuts – who has money to throw away on a new TV, right? But when we broke up it was all so miserable that I just wanted a totally clean slate, a new start. I can't face seeing things every day that remind me of him. Oh – a few notable exceptions. I was hardly going to leave him all my DVDs,' she said, smiling.

'Never.'

There was a glassiness to her eyes that belied the smile.

She misses him. Appearances can be deceptive.

'It's great to have a new start,' Amber said.

That was when I knew I had to make sure hers was a good one.

'What about you? Are you seeing anyone?'

I shook my head. 'I'm better at being single.'

I went to my room and left Amber to unpack the few things she'd brought. I thought about what she'd asked.

I didn't long for romance – God no. I didn't need to be taken out of real life – real life was good. I was happy with real life. But occasionaly I wondered if there was potential for it to be better. I guess, when I put the largely unexamined material of my emotions under the microscope, well maybe there was a little part of me that wanted to know what everyone was talking about. Because I'd never had any cartoon bluebirds follow me through the park, never had that stereo playing out beneath my bedroom window, never had any meaningful encounters at the top of the Empire State, or even got a Valentine's card from anyone apart from Lila (and yes, I wish she wouldn't do that). I knew what it was to care but not to be the centre of someone else's world.

Sam had always been there – at every birthday since I was fifteen. I thought of the book he gave me for one of the birthdays in my late twenties that I'd ended in vodka-fuelled contentment sleeping on his shoulder: *One Day*. As I'd read it, following the story of two friends, not a world away from the two of us, the gift seemed like a kind of promise.

It embarrassed me that he could break through my emotional barriers, even though we were miles apart and out of touch now. I loved the bones of him; more than that, he was part of me. Which was why it wasn't straightforward. Thinking of Sam didn't bring up one simple emotion but many, interlaced and inextricable. I couldn't see, from this close proximity which one was true. I knew what I wanted to believe – that everyone has a soulmate, and Sam was mine, and like something out of a film we would get together in the end. The soundtrack would be a mix CD of the nineties songs we'd listened to in his room, and that we played from my stereo in the skate park. All of the props were ready. The story was ready for filming. It was just that Sam didn't want it to happen, not the way that I did.

Chapter 5

I was coming home after an evening of working late, and jazz music trickled down the steps to the flat. When I got upstairs, I found Amber sitting at a stool in the kitchen, stirring some cake mixture.

'Hey, there,' I said, calling out to her. She smiled and turned down the volume on the iPod dock. 'What are you making?'

'Chocolate and raspberry torte,' she said. 'Fancy some when it's finished?'

'God yes,' I said, settling down on the sofa. 'Thank you.'

'How was work?' Amber asked.

'OK,' I said. After I'd sorted Emma's expenses – a muddle of receipts and scrawled notes that she needed changed into cash 'urgently', Josh and I had stayed talking through potential locations.

'I've flagged up a brilliant place to film with the locations department and I'm really hoping they'll choose it. A country manor down in Sussex.'

'Sounds interesting.' She paused for a moment. 'You know, Hazel, I'm sorry about—' Amber glanced down. 'One of the other assistants mentioned something the other day. About how Tim's job . . . Well, how you have been due a promotion for a while.'

'Don't worry about it,' I said. 'It's hardly your fault.'

'No, but it doesn't seem right. It really doesn't. I can see how much everyone there respects you and your work.'

'This stuff happens,' I said, 'It's starting to dawn on me that maybe, in spite of what she's said, it kind of suits Emma having me where I am.'

'She seems to rely on you a lot.'

'She's been going through a difficult time.' And it had been going on for nearly a year, I thought. I didn't want to dwell on the topic much longer. I wanted to try and stay positive about it all. 'How are you settling in, anyway?'

'It's good,' Amber said. 'In some ways not that different really, given that Tim and I have been working together for years. People seem nice. Money's crap, of course, but nothing new there.'

'Yep. And there are perks, obviously . . .' I said, the same thing I'd been saying to myself since I started.

'Yes. Of course,' Amber said.

'But it would be nice not to have to get Value orange juice

once in a while, maybe splash out on a top that wasn't from H&M?'

'Exactly.' She nodded, laughing. 'And sometimes I wonder if it might be fun to do something else, on the side. Talking of that, how's the wedding planning going?'

Amber had caught me more than once, the glow of my iPad still strong at two or three in the morning as I scoped out venues and dresses for Lila's wedding. Even with the late notice, I'd found a couple of really interesting places where ceremonies could be conducted – the one my heart was set on was the ballet school where she'd first had dance lessons. I was waiting to hear back from them on availability.

'I'm sure you'll do a brilliant job,' Amber said, taking the wooden spoon from the mixture and passing it to me. I dipped my finger into the remaining mixture and tasted it – indulgent and sweet, with layers of flavour. Pretty near perfect. I nodded my approval. I thought of what she'd just said and felt the sudden weight of responsibility.

'Thank you. I'm hopeful I can give her and Ollie the wedding they want. But that doesn't mean I'm not terrified, obviously.'

Amber smiled warmly, and I started to laugh. As I did, I felt the tension that had been building up over the past week start to slip away. And the flat – maybe, just maybe, it was starting to feel like home again.

*

The following Friday night, I went around for dinner at Ollie and Lila's mews house, a short walk from my place, down the main street and then onto a cobbled alleyway. I knocked on the door and Lila ushered me inside. Ollie's place had always been nice, even when Ollie was living there with his best friend – and soon to be best man, Eliot, and the only real furniture they had was a black faux-leather sofa. But with Lila's decorative touches, it had turned into a beautiful, stylish home. Lila had decorated the living room with black and white prints of her favourite ballets and musicals, and cornflowers in antique apothecary bottles on the window sills and open shelving added a splash of colour.

Ollie dished up sea bass with a mango and watercress salad. 'Here you go, Hazel. Thanks for stepping in and saving us, by the way.'

'It's a pleasure,' I said, with a smile.

Lila passed me the guest list to look over. 'Here are the people we want to invite.'

'This is final?' I asked them, taking a sip of cool white wine as my eyes drifted over the long list of names.

'Oh, and the other side too,' Lila said, pointing to the paper.

I flipped it over to see another half-page of names.

'It's practically final, yes.' Ollie said. 'Eliot you know, right?'

I nodded. I'd met Ollie's best man a couple of times, and

he happened to work at the same city bank as Ben. I still found it slightly mind-boggling, how a city could be so big, and so small at once.

'Well he and his fiancée Gemma will be on the top table too. You said you might want to add a couple of people, didn't you, Lila?'

'I'm thinking about it,' she said. 'Rehearsals have just brought me really close to a couple of the other dancers, Raoul and Adele, and I think I'd like to invite them, if we have space, plus ones for both.'

I tore my attention away from the extremely long list, and working out what I was going to do about it, for a moment.

'So things are going well with the show?' I asked.

'There's such a friendly atmosphere,' Lila enthused, 'and the director knows how to get the best from everyone.'

'Great. Right, so I'll pencil in Raoul and Adele, and then in terms of what you've already got, that's, erm . . .' I did a quick mental calculation, then scribbled down the result. 'One hundred and sixty adults and twenty children.' I shook my head. 'This isn't good. None of the venues on my short-list will fit that many people.'

'One hundred and sixty?' Lila gawped. 'I didn't realise it was that many.'

Ollie turned to her. 'We said we didn't even want a big wedding.'

'I know,' she agreed. 'And we don't. Perhaps I should have added up as we went along. God, how did it come to that many?'

'Well, you've given Mum and Dad plus eight, and there are all of Grandma Joyce's neighbours on here too.'

'Maybe cut that back a bit,' Lila said. 'I must have been in a really generous mood when I wrote that.'

'We were a couple of glasses of wine down, I think,' Ollie added.

'And you've got Brandy and Graham, from the village library. Do you really need them there?'

'They've known us since we were tiny,' Lila protested. 'I mean how could I not . . .'

'And the optician?'

'I've always liked him.' She smiled.

I went through the list with my pencil, drawing a thick line through the names of anyone I felt didn't absolutely have to be there. Lila reached out a hand to stop me but I shooed her away. This was a cruel-to-be-kind moment, if ever I saw one.

'Last thing. Is Ben going to use his plus one?' I asked tentatively.

'I don't know if he's even coming himself, yet,' Lila said, looking hurt.

'OK. Well, we'll deal with that one later. We can pare this down a lot with just the people we've already discussed.'

'Oh God, though,' Lila said, her brow creased with concern. 'We're bound to upset someone.'

'They'll understand. It's for the greater good,' I told her. 'I've seen your budget and it's not going to stretch to this, not even if you have it in the community centre.'

'We're not doing that,' Lila said, horrified.

'Of course we're not.'

'One hundred and ten,' I said proudly, passing the list to them. Lila and Ollie read through it, nodding and sharing the occasional anxious look.

'I'm happy if you are,' Ollie said, looking at Lila.

'Just take it,' Lila said, passing it back. 'Don't let me look at it again. It's got to be all about quick decisions, I know that.'

'Brilliant,' I said, with satisfaction. 'Can I show you the invites now?'

'Yes, please,' Lila said, the smile returning to her lips.

I took one last glance at the list before putting it away and a name jumped out at me. I don't know how I'd missed it the first time.

My breath caught, and my chest felt tight.

Then a trace of hope rose up in me filling my lungs with light – that damned hope that stopped me drawing a line under the whole messy thing.

Sam was on the list.

'You're inviting Sam?' I asked, trying to sound nonchalant.

'We were planning to ask him to the evening do,' Lila said.

'Is that awkward? We don't have to, I mean, if it would make you feel uncomfortable.'

'No,' I reassured her.

'Why, who's Sam?' Ollie asked, his interest piqued.

'No one,' I said quietly.

'Hazel's best friend from home,' Lila said. 'We saw him from a distance when we were back in Bidcombe. She made a pass at him last Christmas—'

'LILA,' I snapped, furious.

'Sorry, that came out wrong,' Lila said.

Ollie held his hands up, embarrassed. 'I'm sorry I asked. Forget I mentioned it.'

Silence fell, and Lila glanced down, her cheeks flushed.

'It was a long time ago,' I explained to Ollie. 'And I'm sure – if we do see each other at the wedding – everything will be completely back to normal. It was one drunken moment, that's all.'

Lila's gaze met mine, urging me to accept her unspoken apology.

'We don't have to invite him,' she said. 'We really don't. It's just . . . I've known him a long time, but I guess only through you.'

'Of course he should come,' I said. 'Can I put this away now?' I held the list up. 'No more changes?'

'Sure,' Ollie nodded.

I put it away in my wedding folder. Next to it was a

collage of different cake ideas. 'How about we talk about something altogether more interesting? The cake. Or should I say cakes – because it always seems strange to me that on such an important day you'd only celebrate with one.'

Ollie smiled. 'Now, I've had a few ideas about this.'

Chapter 6

I glanced at the space I'd allocated in my diary for today, Sunday: Wedding Cake day.

I made some breakfast and sat at the kitchen table with my French toast, fruit and coffee, browsing the websites of the country's most highly respected wedding bakers. Traditional tiered cakes vied for my attention alongside rich, indulgent gateaux, minimalist macaroon towers and delicate, delectable-looking French tarts and pastries. Cakes were the make or break element in a wedding, as far as I was concerned – they had the power to turn a day from great into absolutely unforgettable. Then I looked at some of the prices, and my happy helium balloon leaked a little air.

'I could do that,' Amber said, reading over my shoulder. 'That one would be fairly easy.'

She jabbed her finger at the screen, pointing to a layered chocolate and raspberry cake, laden with forest fruits.

I looked up at her. 'I didn't realise you were awake already. Do you want some French toast? I can whip up some more, if you'd like.'

'No – don't worry. I've already had breakfast,' she said. 'But I'm serious, Hazel. This is for your sister's wedding, right? They shouldn't throw their money away on that stuff. They all just whack on an extra fifty per cent when you mention the word wedding, and you don't get anything for it. I could make her an incredible cake. Actually so could you, come to think of it.'

Now Amber mentioned it, perhaps it was worth considering. I'd just had confirmation that the ballet school had availability in August, for the date Lila and Ollie wanted. The only down point was that the elegant venue was going to eat into Lila and Ollie's savings considerably. But there were cutbacks we could make elsewhere, and perhaps this was one of them.

'Fancy a Sunday bake-off?' I dared Amber. 'We could both give it our best shot and then I'll invite Lila and Ollie around to taste?'

'You're on,' Amber said.

Amber chose a disco playlist on her iPod and pulled her dark hair up into a ponytail, pushing her glasses up her nose. 'Right, H. Are you ready?'

I did up the straps on my apron and double-checked the

equipment I had on the kitchen counter. Pablo leapt up onto the kitchen counter and I moved him off, scolding him gently.

'We've got two hours, start to finish, right?' I asked.

'That's right.'

'OK, ready as I'll ever be. Let's go.'

'Car Wash' played out from the speakers and Amber and I got to work, whisking and scooping, stirring and scraping. We worked beside each other, and although we were barely talking, it was relaxed and companionable. It wasn't living with my sister – and it never would be. But I was starting, in small ways, to enjoy it. Incidentally, that did not mean I was going to let her win. No way.

I tried to resist the temptation to look over at what she was doing, but sometimes it proved too much. She seemed to be doing something incredibly complicated with meringue and one of those caramel-gold sugar cages over blueberries.

I'd gone for a light lemon and poppyseed, and the more I looked at it, rising gently in the oven, the more convinced I was that I'd made totally the wrong choice. I'd opted for something that my sister might feasibly take a bite of but it just wasn't celebratory enough. It said Tuesday, Thursday, not – the Biggest and Best Day of your Life. When I got it out of the oven my faith was restored a tiny bit, as my nostrils met with the sweet, enticing aroma. Perhaps something could be simple, but be special too.

I put the cake on a wire rack to cool, standing back for a moment to get some perspective on my effort.

'Ta-da,' Amber said quietly, smiling as she pointed to her cake.

I turned and took in her creation – swirls of meringue meeting glazed berries, linked with delicate wires of spun sugar, tier on tier. It was a dream of a wedding cake. It was a vision.

'Amber,' I said. 'I think you've just knocked this one out of the park.'

By the time Lila and Ollie arrived I was entirely sure my cake didn't stand a chance next to Amber's creation. Hers wasn't just a cake – it was art.

'I'm afraid Amber's pipped you to the post,' Ollie said, licking his spoon.

'Yours was delicious, too, Hazel,' my sister said, 'but I agree with Ollie – Amber, you've got a real talent for this.'

My pride was taking a bit of a hit. Baking was something I'd always considered myself pretty OK at. I hadn't expected to be baking Lila and Ollie's wedding cake – that was always going to be out of my league – but it was my *thing*. Now Amber was better than me at it, a lot better.

'Where did you learn to bake like this?' Ollie asked politely, reading my mind. Amber and I had talked about all sorts of things at work and yet, strangely never this. I'd assumed she was self-taught, like me.

'I have to admit I've had a bit of an advantage,' she said. 'My mum runs a cake shop. She trained me up.'

'Now you tell me,' I said, turning to her with a smile.

'I know. Naughty of me really,' she said. 'But I was in the mood for a bake-off and I didn't want you backing out.'

'Where's the shop?' Lila asked.

'In Sherbourne, near my family home. I grew up with ovens full of delicious baking smells, and last-minute panics as Mum got cakes ready.'

I saw a flicker of concern pass over my sister's face, and the corners of her mouth turned down.

'Don't worry, Lila.' I reassured her. 'That won't happen with you.'

'Of course it won't.' Amber said, confidently. 'It's all in the planning.'

Ollie and Lila looked at each other and appeared to silently agree on something, in that telepathic way they'd developed. That communication that was meant to be exclusive to twins and yet she now seemed to have with him.

'Would you do it, Amber?' Lila said. 'Would you be able to make our cake? We'd love it if you could.'

Someone once told me that the best business-people are the ones who are willing to take on staff who are more gifted than they are. Who can put their pride aside. I reminded myself of that. Having Amber on the team could be the best thing that ever happened for Lila's wedding.

Amber looked at me, gauging my reaction.

'Of course you should do it,' I said.

Amber smiled broadly. 'Great!'

Chapter 7

On Monday, back in the office, Amber and I laid out the remainder of the cake samples in the kitchen at work. Word rapidly got around and people drifted up from their desks, taking slices and stopping to chat as the kettle boiled.

'This is incredible,' Josh said, taking a slice of lemon drizzle.

'Thanks,' I said. 'Glad you like it.'

'You two have something here, I think.'

'Thank you.'

'If I were planning a wedding . . .' He let the sentence trail off.

'Are you?'

'No,' he said hurriedly. 'I mean well, maybe some day. If my family get their way.'

'Well. Bear us in mind,' I said. 'Although by the time that happens I'm confident you won't be able to afford us.'

'A little bit to the left,' Emma said, watching as I accessorised the set for *Christmas at the Manor* later that day. 'Nope – back to the right.'

I took a breath and moved the candlestick back where I had put it in the first place. As I did so, I felt someone looking at me and glanced up to meet Josh's eye. He was standing over by the doorway, and smiled, giving a quick wink of solidarity as I followed Emma's increasingly inconsistent instructions.

'That's it, perfect!' Emma pronounced.

Josh made a face and I stifled the laughter bubbling up inside me.

'Now – the picture frames. I think they're still not quite right,' Emma said.

Josh took a step forward and laid a hand gently on my boss's shoulder. 'You know what, Emma – I see what you're saying. Why don't you step in yourself and make sure they are right. OK if I borrow Hazel for a minute?'

I suspected that Josh didn't need anything from me, but was grateful for the get-out – I'd been following Emma's whims since eight in the morning, and it was starting to grate. In any case, Emma didn't seem to have noticed anything amiss at all, she was focused on unhooking the pictures

I'd got from a nearby antiques market and putting them up in a different arrangement.

'Thanks,' I said, once I was out of earshot. 'I needed a break.'

'I just wanted to say – the location you suggested is perfect. Listen, I know how hard you've been working on the sets, too, and they really do look fantastic. I'll put in a good word for you with Aaron, see if we can't get you some more of the kind of projects you want to be working on.'

'Thank you,' I said.

'I mean – with the promotion going to Tim, and Amber coming in, I guess you probably aren't feeling that motivated.'

I gave a weak smile. 'You could say that.'

'I don't blame you. But let's see if we can't change things, at least a bit. No one wants to lose your talent around here, least of all me.'

At home that evening, I was putting together pictures of flower arrangements for Lila and Ollie's wedding.

'Roses for a wedding, right?' I said.

'I guess,' Amber said, tilting her gaze upwards as if she might find the answer on the ceiling. 'Everyone seems to have roses.'

'Classic, traditional.' I pulled a few images together, with a choice of palettes, as Lila and Ollie hadn't made a final decision on the colour-scheme yet. I'd put together a few pretty options.

'You seem to be really enjoying this,' Amber said. 'I wouldn't have had you pegged as the wedding-y kind.'

'I know what you mean. I guess I've always been a bit of a tomboy. But yes, I really am enjoying it. I mean it's lovely to be asked – and to be part of Lila's day. But it also feels like something I might be good at. It's not really a world away from set designing, after all.'

'I guess not. You look happy.'

'I suppose I feel like you do when you're baking.'

'It's the best feeling in the world. I mean work's OK – there are things about it I really like, and Tim's kind of cool, as bosses go . . . but if I could bake all day? Well, that would be heaven.'

Amber's eyes lit up as she spoke.

'Why don't you?' I suggested. 'I mean, you've got the family business and everything. I bet your mum would be up for it.'

'Going into business together?' Amber said. She shook her head and laughed. 'Oh, I don't know. I love Mum to bits, but I think we'd most likely drive each other mad. She'd be rearranging the sugar decorations and whatnot.'

'Is she really that bad?'

'Ha!' Amber said. 'Yes. I mean she's lovely – but yes, she is that bad. She can be a real perfectionist. And while she'll experiment to a point – she's still pretty traditional. Most of her customers are over sixty, so it's not really in her interest to break with that.'

'You could always set up on your own,' I suggested.

'You make it sound so easy,' she said, with a smile. 'But wouldn't you rather have a flatmate who can pay the rent?'

I smiled. 'I suppose so. Although perhaps the cakes would make up for that.'

She laughed. Then, as we fell quiet again, her gaze trailed over to the window. She'd seemed distracted these past few days, and I asked her what was up.

'Jude called me the other day,' Amber said, trying and failing to look like she didn't care. 'My ex.'

'What did he say?'

'Oh, that he's sorting himself out.' She shook her head. 'That he made a mistake not showing me how serious he was. That he misses me.'

'Do you believe him?'

'Yes. I do. The thing is, I kind of always knew that he needed a wake-up call like this – that it would take me moving out for him to see what he was letting go of. But now that he has . . .'

'Too late? I've closed that door.'

Amber nodded. 'But it's too little, too late. I need to move on now.'

'Do you feel ready to start dating again?'

'I think so. I don't know. I'm not sure I'll ever feel more ready, if that makes sense. I guess I just need to get back on the horse, go for it. It's not about Jude any more, it's not about showing him what he's missing . . . that time's over. It's about finding someone who genuinely appreciates me.'

'You will.' I was more determined than ever to help Amber on her way.

Chapter 8

It was early May, three months before Lila and Ollie's summer wedding, and I'd come to Lila's house to talk through the flowers. I'd gone for pink and white roses. But Lila wrinkled her nose – it might have been barely perceptible to someone else, but to me it was a clear sign of her discontent. 'It's not that I don't like them,' she said. 'I think they're beautiful. And very weddingy. I guess they just don't really seem like what I pictured.'

'And what did you picture?' I asked.

She shook her head, and bit her lip. 'I don't really know. But something, I don't know. Different from this.'

She was right to resist, of course, and it was a niggling feeling I'd been trying to push aside as I'd designed the bouquets and table arrangements. If her wedding were a theatre set it would be perfect, I'd put it together so that all the elements worked in harmony and the final image was one that would bring both beauty and elegance to the day. But this wasn't a theatre set, or a film set.

This was my twin sister's wedding, and even though I knew her inside-out, there was nothing personal about the arrangements I was suggesting.

Lila looked at me from her place on the window seat in her and Ollie's flat, a blank, slightly disappointed expression on her face. I could read her like a book. 'I guess I just never really thought I'd have roses on my wedding day, that's all.' She shrugged, clearly as frustrated by her inability to visualise and communicate exactly what she wanted as I was at not being able to conjure it up for her. My fear was that she would start to have regrets about delegating responsibility for her big day, that she would begin to wonder if getting me involved had been the right thing in the first place.

'I think I get it,' I said. Seeing that look on her face had only made me feel more strongly that I wanted to be part of her day, and to get things right.

With a dash of reluctance, I put aside the vision that I'd carefully concocted, and that had seemed so perfectly, unapologetically, weddingy. I started to refocus on Lila – the brave and sensitive girl and friend I'd spent so much of my life with. I thought back to Lila and how she had been as a child. Warm summer's evenings where I'd be digging something up in the flowerbeds near the kitchen, helping

Dad to plant herbs, and Lila would be wandering through the long grass and the tangle of poppies and wildflowers at the back of Mum and Dad's garden, in a white cotton dress, putting letters out there for the flower fairies. She'd stayed up late the night before, writing the letters at the wooden desk in our shared room, and I'd told her it was a waste of time.

She'd turned to me, her pursed lips forming a perfect red bow, her cheeks lightly flushed with annoyance.

'They won't write back,' I'd grumbled, pulling the duvet up towards my chin and turning over to try and go to sleep. 'They're not even real.'

'They are real. I've seen them,' Lila insisted. 'And I don't mind at all if they don't write back. I just want them to know that someone believes in them. That I believe in them.'

'I bet if they do exist they wouldn't even be able to read and write anyway,' I said. I guess I was the more cynical of the two of us, even then.

She didn't say anything then, just turned her head, with its halo of fluffy blonde hair, knotted from the day's adventures on the grass, and brought her attention back to the letter she was writing. I pretended my eyes were closed, but actually I watched her until I finally fell asleep. I watched as she paid painstaking attention to the shape and curl on each letter she was writing. Her handwriting was something she was very proud of, and in truth I envied her for it. I envied her too for her capacity to believe in things that had long stopped seeming plausible to me.

The following Monday, when Lila was gathering her things together for school, packing her dance shoes and outfit, something I didn't have to think about, I found Dad upstairs in the bathroom shaving, with that noisy electric shaver he used to use.

I snuck in behind him and when he sensed me he jumped a little. 'Hazel, hi. You startled me.' His face broke into a wide smile. Dad had one of those smiles that made you feel that the world was a good place. Mum smiled a lot, but sometimes the sad things that she saw and heard about crept through, and those smiles she gave out didn't make you feel as safe as Dad's did.

Anyway, Dad and I were standing there in the bathroom, with the whale-print wallpaper that I had insisted we get for it, and mine and Lila's fluffy purple towels on our pegs on the walls, and I knew I had a chance to make things right, to make up for the way I'd been mean to Lila at the weekend. Because she deserved to carry on believing. It was a nice thing to be able to do.

'What is it, love?' Dad asked, kindly.

'Dad, you have to do something,' I said, certain now, of the action I must take. I took a deep breath. 'You have to be the fairies.'

Mum called out again for us to get ready, so I knew I

didn't have long to brief Dad on what he needed to do, but I managed to give him the general idea. I knew he had it in him, deep down, to be a superhero, and being a fairy was really quite a lot easier than that.

That evening, when we got back from school, my dad had winked at me – confirmation that he'd done what we'd discussed and that everything was ready. As I'd expected, my sister ran into the back garden and out to the long grass and wildflowers, her hands rifling through the flowers and weeds with determination and a sense of focus. This time I followed her over there, standing back a bit on the lawn, but close enough to watch the scene unfold.

As she located the wild patch of foxgloves and poppies where she'd placed her letter, she let out a whoop of glee. 'They came!' she shouted over to me. Her green eyes were wide and shining with excitement as she held up the card, with her name – LILA – written in purple ink.

'They did?' I said, smiling. 'Well, bring it over here, then. Let's open it together.' With a spring in her step, Lila came over to where I was sitting, and gingerly fingered the sealed envelope. 'Perhaps we should tell someone,' she said.

'Like Mum?'

'No,' she shook her head. 'I don't know. Is there a fairy society? Natural History Museum maybe? I don't think this is common, you know,' Lila continued earnestly.

'I think it's OK for us to keep it secret,' I replied. 'Anyway, let's open it first and see what it says. It might not even be from them.'

'It IS,' Lila said, confidently. 'I just know it is.'

Inside was a pretty card with a picture of a fairy on it, and a neatly written note. Dad had clearly worked hard to disguise his handwriting, and while you could still tell, a little bit, Lila didn't seem to notice, or was choosing not to.

Dear Lila, it read. *Thank you for believing in us. It means an awful lot. We always enjoy your visits to our home, this part of the garden, even though most of the time we hide from you. Don't take it personally. It's just what fairies do. You're very big, compared to us, after all, so there's always the risk of being trampled on — or, well, you telling someone about us.*

'Like the Natural History Museum,' I chimed in. Helpful like that. Lila nodded. 'You were right,' she said. 'We need to keep this a secret.'

'How did they sign off?' I asked, genuinely curious.

'Love, Your friends, the fairies.'

I smiled. Dad had excelled himself. Lila clutched the card to her chest and smiled broadly. 'It's the most, most special thing that's ever happened to me,' she said. 'I'm going to write back to them right away.'

'You were right to believe after all, I guess.'

'I was,' she said, proudly.

Over the course of that summer, Dad must have written

to Lila a dozen times. As the autumn leaves began to fall, and Ben and I raked them in the September sunshine, Lila got her last letter from her friends in the garden.

'They're flying south for the winter,' she explained to me. 'They said they need to do that, like birds.' She shrugged as if it were nothing but I could see her eyes shining with unshed tears. 'I didn't actually know that about them. But it makes sense. They say they'll have to go to another garden next summer. That's how it works I suppose. They can't stay with us for ever.'

I glanced over at Dad, and caught his eye for a split second, but then he looked back down at the rake he was holding. Beside him, Ben was sweeping piles of cut grass up in his hands, and letting it fall around him, letting out a gurgle of toddler laughter.

It seemed harsh but I knew Dad had done the right thing. Even Lila couldn't go on believing forever. This gave both of them a way out.

That evening, I went downstairs for some water, and overheard Dad talking to Mum in the kitchen. 'We should do something for Hazel,' he said. 'Something special. Like the fairies.'

'Oh no, Simon,' Mum said, laughing lightly. 'There's no need. She's not dreamy like Lila. You know as well as me, they're quite different.'

'A surprise, though . . .' he said, mulling it over.

'I don't think so, Simon,' Mum said. 'Hazel's always been happier looking after the others; she's not one to be made a fuss of. Let's just be grateful for that – she'll always be our easy child ...'

Lila coughed, and my attention was brought back into the room. She was looking down at my iPad and the Pinterest boards I'd put together for her, and frowning slightly.

'They're not right for you. I can see that now,' I said. Her relief showed immediately, the lines between her brows smoothed out, her shoulders went from hunched to relaxed.

'What about wildflowers?' I suggested, drawing the images from our childhood memories back into my mind. 'Poppies and marguerites ... We could put them on each table, use some of the lovely apothecary bottles you have, I can easily source some more, string them up around the venue ...' I rattled through the other ideas, coming to me quickly and easily now. I could picture the scene perfectly.

Lila paused for a moment, and then began to smile. The light came back into her eyes. 'Like in our garden?' she said, remembering.

'Yes, just like that,' I replied.

'I think that's a wonderful idea.'

Chapter 9

It was late on Friday evening, and the office had emptied out. It was just me and Josh left, working on a new set design for *Christmas at the Manor*. Josh looked over my ideas – a lavish pine tree in the living room and tall red candles with frosted white holders on the table. The residents of the manor were rich and not afraid to show it, which was a dream when it came to designing their Christmas decorations.

'Have you got some starting points for sourcing this stuff?' Josh said. 'It looks fantastic, by the way.'

I smiled, and showed Josh the list that I'd drafted. 'I've got a few quotes.'

'OK, that looks good. Can I show you the ideas I've had for the village pub?'

The village pub was the heart of the community, and where most of the drama took place. The residents of the manor would rarely set foot in it, so it was also the perfect forum for people to discuss them – and where the best gossip came out.

Josh showed me his sketches of the pub – the cosy fireside where the village dogs stretched out to warm up after long, snowy walks, the mirror strung with fairy lights and the mistletoe hanging down from the beams of the seventeenth-century building. I thought back to the script we'd been given, and pictured Elise and Joey, two of the show's most popular characters, under there. Everyone knew that the audience were going to go wild when they saw these two finally pair up – all that was needed was the perfect set for the encounter.

'I can make that,' I said. 'There's no way that Elise is going to be able to resist Joey over mulled wine on Christmas Eve.'

'Fantastic. Look – talking of pubs. I'm meeting Sarah in half an hour, at the Railway. Why don't you join us? It's about time you guys met – I think you'd get on.'

'Great,' I said. So, I'd finally get to meet the woman Josh was in love with. This felt like a big deal.

Out of season, there was no mulled wine, but between us, and over two glasses of red, Josh and I began to conjure up the spirit of Christmas in a booth in the corner of the Railway.

He glanced at his phone. 'Sarah's running late. Which is pretty standard. She kind of runs on her own time.' He smiled, and didn't seem particularly bothered by it.

'Cool,' I said. 'No hurry.'

'I like this place,' Josh said, glancing around. 'Right in the heart of London but it feels almost like a countryside local, doesn't it?'

'Yes. Reminds me a bit of home, actually.' I thought of the pub, on our village green. Lila and I had had to wait patiently for our eighteenth birthday, with the landlord being one of Dad's best friends, there wasn't a chance that we'd be let in underage – but it made it even more special when we were finally allowed to spend the evening there.

I came back to the moment, Josh watching me with a smile on his lips. 'Where did you go to just then?'

'Oh, nowhere,' I said, uneasy that I'd been caught day-dreaming. 'Well, eighteen years old, if you must know.'

'Good memories?'

I mulled over the question.

'Some,' I said.

'Weird time, isn't it, being a teenager? I can't say I look back on it very nostalgically. Twenties were a lot better. And thirties seem to be shaping up to be better still.'

'You're happiest now?' I asked.

'Definitely.' And he looked it – content, relaxed in his own skin. 'I think that's why I met Sarah now. When I was ready to meet her.'

Right then, she arrived.

Sarah seemed to float into the pub. She wore a strapless dress wound out of turquoise sari fabric, and leather sandals, despite the drizzly weather. Her long, wavy hair was loose, and she had faint freckles on her shoulders.

Josh kissed her hello and introduced us. There was a twinkle of mischief in her wide blue eyes.

'Hi,' I said, holding out my hand to greet Sarah. She laughed and instead came in close to kiss me on the cheek. Her hair was soft and smelled of honey.

'Great to finally meet you,' she said brightly. 'Josh has told me so much about you.'

'He has?'

'Oh yes, loads. Good stuff, obviously.'

I smiled.

'Said you've got a sideline in wedding planning at the moment?'

'Kind of. Only informally. I'm planning my sister's wedding at the moment. Their wedding planner bailed on them, so I've stepped in.'

'Your sister's wedding – how sweet,' Sarah said.

'And you work at an art gallery, is that right?'

'Oh I did,' Sarah said, waving her hand, and laughing. 'That didn't last long.' She lowered her voice to a whisper,

'"*Too many opinions*"', they told me. Can you believe it? In the art world of all places? I was brought up to think that having a mind was a good thing.'

Josh smiled. 'Sarah doesn't back down easily.'

Over the course of the evening, that was definitely the impression I got.

Later that week, Lila and I were sitting cross-legged on the rug on the floor of her and Ollie's living room, threading paper chains. They were made from silver paper doilies, so had the appearance of being lacy – delicate and fragile. Or perhaps, on reflection, a bit like a bridal spider web.

'These are going to look gorgeous,' Lila said cheerfully.

'It's all coming together,' I said. And they weren't just words to reassure Lila and calm her pre-wedding jitters. Things really were looking good. The RSVPs had flooded in quickly, and most were yeses.

'Any word from Ben, yet?' I asked.

'Yes, but no firm answer. He left a rambling voicemail. Said he's busy over the summer – work commitments.' She said the words sarcastically. 'I mean, I know we're not that close, but I really thought ... I never imagined that our brother might not be there to see me get married.'

'He has to be there,' I said. 'I'll make sure he is.'

*

The following Saturday, we met Mum at the wedding-dress shop, in a courtyard just behind Columbia Road. It didn't look like much from the outside, but the dressmaker, Jane, who I'd met while researching costumes for the TV company, was creative and practical – perfect for getting my sister the wedding dress she needed, in record time.

Mum hugged us both hello, and then we walked up the narrow spiral staircase together. Jane greeted us at the door, her hair piled on her head and tied with a length of gingham fabric. She had on jeans and a fifties shirt knotted at the waist, and for a moment I sensed Lila stiffen, perhaps doubting whether this was the right person to be designing her dress. But the moment we stepped into the room, Tardis-like in its dimensions, the atmosphere changed. White satin and silk covered the walls, dresses sparkling with diamante and silken embroidery hung on their hangers. Structured bodices, with full, romantic skirts, empire line dresses straight out of *Pride and Prejudice*, and then more unusual designs, one-shouldered and asymmetrical, one with a bright-coloured petticoat and sash.

'Wow,' Lila said, her gaze drifting around the room, taking it all in. A wide smile came to her face. 'This place is a wedding wonderland.'

Jane smiled modestly.

'She's a miracle worker,' I said, familiar with all the work Jane had done for the costume department on tight deadlines. 'And she's going to do a fantastic job on your dress, I promise you.'

'She's being kind,' Jane said. 'Now, why don't you all sit down on the chaise longue, I'll get us some Champagne and we can talk through your ideas.'

Mum smiled, and sat next to my sister on the seat. She nudged Lila gently. 'Well, this is a bit special, isn't it?'

I got out some of the images Lila and I had put together as a collage, and when Jane returned with the drinks, I showed them to her.

'Lila's a dancer, like I mentioned to you on the phone, so I think she'd like something with lightness and grace. Is that right, Lila?'

'Yes. Nothing over-the-top, a top that's lean and I guess a little like a leotard, with a skirt that's floaty and fairy-like. I don't want anything too structured – it's going to be a summer wedding, and I'd like the dress to reflect that.'

'Nice,' Jane said, taking a few notes. 'How do you feel about sparkles?'

'I can do sparkles,' Lila said, with a smile. 'That would be nice. I do want it to feel special, just not, you know, fussy.'

'Perfect. The kind of dress I like best. And you have the kind of figure that could carry anything off, which helps.'

Lila shifted in her seat and looked down at the dark wood floorboards.

'Sorry, I didn't mean to . . .' Jane said, backtracking.

'Do you have anything similar we could take a look at?' I said, jumping in and hurriedly trying to change the subject.

'Yes,' Mum said, clearly feeling the same way, and jumping to her feet, busying herself with looking at some of the gowns that were hanging up. 'This one is gorgeous,' she said, pointing to a knee-length 1920s style dress, with Art Nouveau detailing.

Lila smiled again.

This is what we did, me and Mum, and I'm not sure really why, apart from out of habit. When there was something wrong with Lila, we put all our energies into pretending there wasn't – as if that would make it all go away.

Chapter 10

I turned up the volume on my iPod dock, and sat down at the desk in my room. In front of me were printed images of dresses, flowers and cake, and now it only remained for me to make the set for Lila and Ollie's wedding. I'd constructed the basic shape of the ballet school, and painted it, and now took out a scalpel from my pencil case and cut out the small figures that represented my sister and her groom. Once I had her dress right – following the design we'd discussed with the dress-maker, I got to work on Ollie. Even here, in miniature form, they looked just right together. Ollie had quickly become Lila's anchor, the stability that she needed after years of drifting back and forth to shore. Not that she'd necessarily been unhappy – we'd had a hundred nights of laughing and talking, and having fun in that time, but Lila herself had admitted more than once that she sometimes felt as if she was hovering over herself, looking down. Like she couldn't quite take hold of who she was, be at the steering wheel of her own life. I can't say I understand exactly what she means – it's not something I've ever felt, but I understood well enough to notice that something changed when she met Ollie. Her eyes ceased darting around and her energy was different – she was calmer.

I placed tiny flower arrangements on the tables, and going up the aisle in the dance studio at the ballet school, tiny versions of the wildflower posies that Lila and I had settled on. The wooden benches were filled with paper silhouettes, representing the guests. At the event itself, our family and friends would be on one side, Ollie's on the other. I still hadn't heard from Ben – but I put him in there.

Next, I put Lila and Ollie in place, Ollie waiting at the top of the aisle next to the celebrant, and Lila and the bridesmaids, including me, in a floaty dress, at the doorway of the building in Leamington Spa.

I got to my feet, stood back and took in the scene. From the tealights lighting the way up the stairs, to the flowers wound around the banisters up to the venue, it was taking shape.

A knock came at the door and I hurriedly put the set away in my closet. 'Yes?' I said, closing the door and drawing the latch across it.

Amber put her head around the door. 'You coming out of here tonight? I've made us some pasta, if you're hungry.'

'Sure.' I nodded. 'Thanks.'

'Head full of wedding planning?' Amber guessed.

'A bit,' I said, smiling at the way she always seemed to be able to see right through me. 'I guess it is.'

'Your sister's lucky to have you,' Amber said.

'She deserves for this to go perfectly.'

'Hey,' I said, when Lila picked up the phone later that day. 'What you up to this afternoon? Fancy popping around for tea?'

'Oh, I don't know,' she said, distantly. 'I've got a few things to do at home.'

'Sorting your knicker drawer again?' Lila and Ollie's flat was always immaculate – I didn't believe for a second that there was anything pressing that needed doing.

'Something like that,' she said. There was no accompanying laugh, though, and it was yet another signal to me that I shouldn't give up.

'I'll come to you,' I suggested.

'No,' Lila snapped.

I drew in my breath at her response, and the line fell silent for a moment.

'Sorry,' she said, after a pause. 'I didn't mean to sound unfriendly ... it's just, I'm in the middle of something, like I said.'

'Something so important you don't even have five minutes?' I said, not believing her.

'I can't,' she said. It didn't matter that we were on the phone, I could hear her voice crack.

She hung up.

I sat with the phone still cradled in my hand. Something was wrong.

I couldn't sit back and watch this all happening again. I just couldn't.

Here, in my kitchen, surrounded by the smells of fresh baking and coffee just brewed, I was cast back to our days as teenagers. When Lila was fighting an internal enemy, one that was trying to trip her up as we trod the path of adolescence together.

It should have been obvious to us all that something was wrong a lot earlier than it was. When I visited Lila on the hospital ward, she was only sixteen.

I cycled into work the next day, and found Josh at my desk putting a folder in my in-tray. The office was empty and quiet.

'The new script,' he explained. 'I thought you might want to have a look through.'

'Thanks,' I said.

I felt as if I could barely focus. His face – it was all just a blur – I was seeing Josh with my memory more than with my eyes.

'Hazel, are you OK?' he asked, coming to my side.

I breathed in, trying to calm down. My legs were unsteady and I felt as if I might fall over. He put his arm around me, and led me over to the sofa in Emma's office. I'd spent time with Lila, plenty of time, planning the wedding – and yet I'd totally failed to see that she was unhappy.

I sat down, and the dizziness eased. Josh sat next to me, a look of concern in his eyes. 'That any better?' I nodded mutely.

'You wait there, I'll get you some water.'

He came back a moment later with a glass. I took tentative sips, and the sick feeling started to subside. The usual distance between me and Josh had returned, and he wasn't sitting so close any more. I kind of wanted him to come back.

'You went so pale,' he said.

'Sorry,' I managed at last. 'Felt fine this morning, then it came on all of a sudden when I got here.'

'Shall I call you a cab?' he said, already getting his phone out of his pocket. I stilled his hand with mine. As I touched his warm skin, I felt better. Safer. As if what I had started to suspect was happening to Lila, wasn't. Not really.

'No,' I said. My hand was still there, on his, and neither of us moved to change that. 'I'd rather be here.'

'OK,' he said. I moved my hand back to my lap, and normality crept back in. 'I'll just keep my head down a bit today.' I finished the glass of water in a gulp. 'See, feeling much better already, really. Thanks for that.' I moved to get up, and then my vision blurred again.

'Hazel, what's going on?' Josh said, concerned.

'Must be food poisoning or something,' I lied. He fixed me with a stare that told me he didn't believe me.

'Is it Lila?'

As he said her name, goosebumps rose on the skin of my upper arms, and my legs. I felt as if he could see right through me, and I wasn't used to feeling that way with anyone.

I nodded. Tears welled up in my eyes and I brushed them away hurriedly, as if that way he wouldn't know I was crying.

'What's happened?'

'It's a long story,' I said. 'I'm just a bit worried about her at the moment. I can't shift this feeling.'

'You need to go. Go to her and find out what's going on.'

'But I can't . . .' I said. 'There's too much going on, with Emma, with the show . . .'

'Nothing that can't wait. I'll cover for you, Hazel.'

I walked through the rain-streaked east London streets to Lila's flat. The rosebushes were usually bright with spring blooms, but now the grey city drizzle had reduced them, in their fallen pastel-coloured form, to just another layer of sludge, alongside discarded free newspapers and chocolate wrappers. I skidded a little in my heeled boots, and let loose a swearword. I didn't need to be hurrying – Lila didn't know I was coming, and from the way she was on the phone there was every chance she wouldn't even speak to me, but I felt a sense of urgency in getting there. My gut told me that she wouldn't be at rehearsals today, even though she hardly ever missed them.

I saw the glow of a lamp in Lila's upstairs living room. The same oversized desklight that had once been in our flat, next to the sofa. A figure got up to standing, silhouetted against the window, looking out. The way her chin was slightly lifted, how her hips jutted out slightly from her slim waist. Twelve, or twenty-nine, it was unmistakably Lila.

I let myself in as quietly as I could, with the spare keys, hoping it wouldn't startle her. Now I was here there was no way I was going to risk her ignoring the doorbell and pretending I wasn't there. This way she wouldn't be able to blank me out. She appeared at the top of the stairs in a loose t-shirt and tracksuit bottoms, her hair tied back and her face gaunt. 'Hazel. What are you doing here?' Her voice was faint though, not angry.

'I want us to talk, Lila. And I mean really talk. I don't want to be brushed off any more.'

'OK,' she said, moving slightly to one side at the top of the staircase. 'Come up.'

My heart raced as I walked up the stairs. I'd half-hoped she'd deny that anything was wrong. But she hadn't.

Lila made us tea and we sat together by the window, mugs warming out hands. As the rain fell more heavily outside, you could almost forget for a moment that it was supposed to be summer.

'You shouldn't have sneaked in like that,' she reprimanded me.

'Maybe not.' I shrugged. Her face was strained, and there was a greyness to her skin. It pulled tight across her forehead and cheeks.

I made myself say it. 'I was worried about you, Lila. I *am* worried about you.'

'Don't be,' she said, flatly. She looked down at the floor and scuffed at a whorl in the floorboard with the toe of her slipper. 'I'm fine.'

'No you're not.'

Our gazes met, and I saw that the bottom rims of Lila's eyes were a deep red.

'You look exhausted,' I said.

'Rehearsals have been busy.'

'Come on, it's not just that.' I took a breath. 'Lila. Be honest with me. What's really going on?'

The room fell quiet. I searched Lila's face for the familiar clues – the way her gaze would dart away from mine, or the side of her bottom lip would disappear into her mouth as she bit it, the way her eyebrows would come together just a fraction and a faint line would appear between them.

'Nothing,' she said. She shook her head. 'Nothing's wrong at all.'

And with those words, she shut the conversation down. But I'd seen it, that tiny crease in her brow that told me she was lying.

As I walked home on my own, I remembered how it had been, back then.

She looked so small in the hospital bed, beneath the white sheets and the pastel-coloured blanket. Her arms were thin, pale as her face.

'You came,' Lila said, her voice quieter than usual.

'Of course I came, you divvo,' I said.

In spite of her evident discomfort, she smiled then, at my familiar insult. Just a whisper of a turn at the corner of her lips, but I saw it, and it lifted my heart.

'Boring as hell in here,' she said. 'Mum and Dad brought me the lamest magazines, and while I've swapped them with the other patients, I can't say it really worked out that well for me.' She pointed over at a copy of Dogs UK *magazine, and there it was again, a glimmer of the sister I knew.*

'You'll be out soon,' I said, taking a seat. I said it brightly. Because it was true, surely. This was Lila we were talking about, not one of those unhappy teenagers who get caught up in wanting to look thin. She wasn't like that. Plus everyone fancied her − all of the

*boys at school. There was no way she could feel that she wasn't
attractive.*

'I hope so,' Lila said.

'You will,' I said.

'Thanks for being here,' she said. 'It's kind of lonely.'

'I guess it must be,' I said, looking around at the adult ward.

*'I don't like the quiet. Not really,' Lila said. 'Because when it's
quiet, I hear it all more.'*

'Hear what?' I asked, nervously.

'The bad stuff.'

*'Don't,' I said, covering her delicate, frail hand with my own.
'You're going to be OK, you know.'*

*Lila's eyes filled with tears. 'Am I? I feel like I'm a hundred years
old right now.'*

'You'll be fine,' I said, telling myself as much as her.

*Lila looked up and her green eyes met mine. There was despera-
tion in her gaze. As if she was reaching out to me to bring her back
up to the surface again. 'Hazel. I need you to understand. I need
you to be different.'*

Chapter 11

The next day at work, Josh caught me in the corridor.

'You OK today, Haze?'

I'd been able to push Lila from my mind for the first hour of the day, but now, with these words from Josh, I felt as if I might cry.

'Yes.' Our eyes met. I gave him the most convincing smile I could muster.

'Come in here a second.' He led me into the empty meeting room and pulled up chairs for us both. From a tin left on the side he produced a biscuit, which I nibbled on gratefully.

'How did it go yesterday?'

'I'm not really sure,' I said. 'I saw Lila. And she says she's fine, but I don't know – I just don't buy it, Josh. I'm worried that the pressure of everything might be getting to her.'

'The wedding?'

'That – and her rehearsals. Lila's a perfectionist, always has been. And when things don't go exactly as she wants them to ...' My voice cracked as I thought about how badly things could go wrong. In over a decade, Lila had, as far as I knew, not had a relapse. She'd seen a counsellor for three years after things got bad, and would still check in a few times a year. But Lila had told me before that it was always there, it never went away, and that she knew one day it could come back.

'I feel like there's nothing I can do,' I said.

'You showed her that you're there for her,' Josh said, reassuringly.

'I guess.' It didn't feel enough.

'Keep showing her.'

I felt tears well in my eyes again and start to spill on to my cheeks. Perhaps the very wedding I was helping to plan was the thing that was causing the problem.

Gently, Josh brushed the tear from my cheek with his thumb.

He'd never been so close to me before, but it felt comfortable. More than comfortable. It felt good.

I spent lunchtime on my own at my desk, sending out invites for Lila's hen night. I'd arranged a workshop making fascinators for the wedding followed by a night out in Soho. It felt a little surreal, making these final preparations for the wedding when my gut told me that there was something going on, something serious enough that it might end up compromising the whole thing.

At around three I went out to the courtyard to get some fresh air, and Josh came over. 'I got you something,' he said. 'I might not be able to fix things for you, but I'm pretty good with distractions.'

He passed me some tickets to an exhibition at the Victoria and Albert Museum, a display of the best sets for musical theatre through the past century. 'They were selling out really quickly, so I thought I'd bike it over there and get them.' I felt comforted by the warmth in his brown eyes.

My face flushed in surprise at the gesture. I'd seen the exhibition advertised and it looked really inspiring. 'Thank you,' I said, taking the tickets he was holding out. 'You didn't need to . . .'

'Entirely selfish really,' Josh said modestly.

'Selfish?'

'Yes,' he said. 'I know I didn't have to. But I don't ever want to see you sad, Hazel.'

My gaze drifted down to his full mouth, and for the briefest of moments, before sense kicked back in, I wondered what it might be like to kiss him.

*

August arrived, sultry and warm, and a hum of activity filled every crevice of the city. Workers cast off their blazers and suit jackets, and used them as makeshift rugs while they spread out in London's green spaces to eat their Pret sandwiches and sushi.

The days passed in a blur. From the final wedding-dress fittings, to confirming details at the venue and stage-managing Lila's hen night, organising the wedding had become a full-time job alongside my full-time job. Lila was caught up in the whirlwind, and seemed to have shaken off the melancholy I'd picked up on in her. We were all excited, and she was too. I didn't ask her again. But I hope I made it clear that if she wanted to talk to me, I was there. We shared late nights together going over the final details, and arranging the playlist.

I enjoyed the whirl of organisation too. Maybe because it helped me to push the feelings that I'd started to have for Josh to one side. They seemed to have come from nowhere, and I was very keen for them to go right back there.

Mum and Grandma Joyce were still clamouring to get more involved, but Lila wanted to keep them at arm's length. We let them loose on the table plan, which they took to with great enthusiasm, and then subtly rearranged a couple of people's places afterwards. Ben RSVPd yes, at long last, and everyone breathed a sigh of relief.

To see Lila at her hen night, surrounded by her best girlfriends and fellow ballet dancers, laughing again, meant everything. It was finally time to see my twin sister get married.

Chapter 12

You are cordially invited to the wedding of

Lila Delaney and Ollie Neal

At: The Ballet School, Leamington Spa

It was the day before the wedding.

'It's easier than it looks, I promise,' Amber reassured me, as I eyed the four separate cakes she'd baked on their individual cooling racks on the counter. We'd settled on a multi-tier affair, with the top layer covered in edible rose petals. I'd begun to wonder if perhaps we'd been a little ambitious.

She lowered the second-largest cake and then, at the last moment, dropped it onto the bottom one. 'See?' she said proudly. If it weren't for the tiniest bead of sweat on her brow

I would have thought she'd had no doubts at all about the success of the manoeuvre.

'Now it's your turn,' she said, pointing to the next-largest cake.

'No – honestly, it's fine,' I said. 'You do it, you did most of the baking, after all – I don't want to mess anything up now.'

'You won't,' Amber said.

She led me over to the cake. All I could picture was Lila and Ollie's wedding, the scene set, everything perfect except for the cake, once beautiful and glistening, and now a patched-up mess after my actions.

Like all the details of Lila and Ollie's day – the cake really mattered. It would be the centrepiece at the reception, and Amber had worked for days getting the design and recipe just right.

I held the cake gently in my hands, and steadied my nerves with a deep breath. With an encouraging nod from Amber, I lifted it. I felt like I had the whole of Lila's wedding in my hands – and it was down to me not to drop it.

Lowering it onto the two bottom tiers seemed to take for ever. Then, at the final moment, just as Amber had done, I let the cake drop. It fell into position and I realised I'd been holding my breath – I let it out as a wave of relief passed over me.

'Hooray,' Amber said, smiling proudly at me, and adding

the top cake, as if it were no effort at all. 'See? I told you so,' she said.

'God,' I said, turning to Amber. 'It's just hit me. How much is at stake.'

'Don't worry.' Her eyes, kind, reminded me that I had an ally, whatever happened tomorrow. 'It's going to go perfectly. Trust me.'

The next day, Amber and I drove up to my family's home with the cake. She'd be coming to the wedding as my plus one, so she'd have a chance to enjoy the party as well. We'd booked Amber into a local B&B, while I stayed at the cottage. That evening, Lila, Mum and I were sitting around the kitchen table. It was the table that had nurtured in Lila and me the desire to have a gathering place in our own homes.

'You look pale, sweetie,' Mum said to Lila, who was nursing a cold cup of tea.

'I'm fine, Mum,' she insisted. With Ollie staying at a hotel that night, I was seeing her on her own for the first time in what felt like months. Mum was right. She looked terrible.

'Last-minute nerves?' Mum asked.

Lila shrugged. 'I guess.'

'It's not too late to back out, you know,' Ben, our little brother, said. From anyone else, it would have been a joke,

111

but from Ben – well. But at least he was here, sitting at the table in a work shirt undone at the collar, and a day's worth of dark stubble. It had taken more than a couple of nudges from me and Mum, but he was here.

'I need some time on my own,' Lila said, getting to her feet. We watched her leave the room, and then heard the front door close behind her.

'She's upset, isn't she?' Dad said. In contrast to my brother, whose default setting seemed to be sneering these days, my Dad is unfailingly kind. 'Shall I go after her?'

I knew if anyone could help Lila relax, it would be Dad. He'd always had a particular skill for calming a situation. We'd joked in the past that he should be a hostage negotiator rather than an accountant, but he'd always insisted that managing our family was front-line enough for him.

'Let's give her a few minutes on her own first,' I said.

'Maybe she's changed her mind, and decided she wants someone who actually earns a living,' Ben said.

'Ollie's a lovely boy,' Mum said.

'Man,' I corrected her.

'Exactly, that's what I said.' She turned to Dad and put her hand on top of his, in that way they had.

'Now, shall I put the kettle on?' Mum said. 'I'll get Lila a cup of peppermint, that should help her when she's back.'

Ben's phone rang and he got to his feet. 'Yes, yes, I'm familiar with them,' Ben said, switching into work mode. I rolled my eyes as he left the room. 'Even now, he's not going to switch that thing off?'

Mum turned to me. 'Go easy on him,' she said. 'It's just a phase. Don't let it wind you up.'

'Just a phase, Mum?' I said. 'He's twenty-five. You shouldn't be making excuses for him – especially not when he's as rude as he was just now about Ollie.'

Mum looked out the window as the kettle boiled, watching the back of Lila's head as she paced slowly up and down outside. 'He'll be all right in a little while. They both will.'

Silence fell between us for a moment.

'You don't think she *has* got cold feet, do you, Hazel?' Mum asked me quietly.

'No.' I shook my head confidently. 'She and Ollie are just as hopelessly in love as always, believe me, I've spent the last few days witnessing it at particularly close quarters.'

'She doesn't seem herself, though,' Mum said.

Of course, I was wondering the same thing, couldn't stop wondering, but I didn't see that it would help anything to let Mum know that.

'All brides get nervous.'

'I suppose,' she said. I could see it in her eyes, the same worry that had been plaguing me.

'Everything will be fine tomorrow,' I said, hoping it would be true.

*

When Lila came back inside, she walked right through the kitchen and up the stairs, barely looking at us.

A few moments later, I followed her. As I'd expected, she was up in the attic, in the corner. It wasn't a proper room, more of a den, the beanbags and cushions we'd sat on as children still strewn around. She must've heard my feet on the floorboards, as she looked up to face me, her face streaked with tears. I sat beside her, my hand gently covering her bare feet.

'What's wrong?' I asked her softly.

'It's not just one thing,' Lila said, her voice cracking. 'I just feel sort of overwhelmed by it all. The pressure, all the people. And what we're doing – Ollie and me. Sometimes it seems like the most natural thing in the world, and then at other times I wonder if we're crazy.'

'You're not. You guys are perfect together,' I reassured her. 'Tomorrow will be beautiful – I can promise you that much. And the rest of your lives – you and Ollie will work that all out.'

'I guess,' she said, forcing a smile.

'Have you been feeling OK?' I enquired gently. 'I mean, it must be difficult, what with the performances, and then all of this . . .'

'Mostly, yes,' she said, and I could see she'd registered what I was really asking. 'I'm not going to pretend it's been easy, there have been moments that I've worried it was happening again. There have been days when thoughts have flickered across my mind and I've had to force them back out. And that's one of the things on my mind. Just because I haven't got sick again, that doesn't mean that I won't. How can I expect Ollie to be there for me, through all of that . . .'

'Because he'll want to be there,' I said. 'I hope it never happens, and with any luck it won't. But if it does – he'll want to be there for you, Lila – just like I did. Just like all of our family did.'

She dried her eyes roughly with the back of her hand, and met my gaze.

'Anyway – who knows how things will pan out, it could just as easily be you that needs to be there for him.'

'I suppose.'

'And isn't that what marriage is supposed to be all about?'

She nodded.

'There's something else, too,' she said. 'Connected to what happened back then.'

She looked more fragile for a moment, as she took herself back there.

'Ollie knows about what happened, but not the full story – nothing about the hospital, or how bad things really got. I didn't want us – this good, happy thing – getting tarnished with the general messed-up-ness of me.'

I shook my head. 'Lila, you shouldn't see it like that . . .'

'Well, I do. I don't want him to think I married him on

false pretences, got him to sign up to a life with me thinking I was sorted, when I'm not . . .'

'I'm sure he wouldn't want you to be anything other than the woman you are.'

'I don't know,' Lila said, welling up. 'On a good day I think that. But now I'm starting to think that that past – the one I've been trying for years to leave behind, might end up being part of our present too. And our future. I was a teenager back then, and what the doctors told me didn't really sink in. Hazel, they said that after everything that happened, all that my body's been through, there was likely to be some permanent damage.'

'Right,' I said. She hadn't mentioned it to me at the time, and perhaps my parents had shielded me from it too.

'Ollie wants a baby. And so, I think, do I. But I'm scared. I'm worried it's not going to happen.'

'Have you told him that?'

She nodded. 'I said I wasn't sure if it would be possible.'

'And what did he say?'

'He says he loves me and wants to be with me no matter what,' Lila said, rubbing away a tear.

'Well, there you go,' I said. 'OK, so things might not be straightforward for you, but no one has any guarantees. You love each other and want to get married – don't let this stand in your way.'

Her eyes met mine, and she took my hand. 'Thank you.'

Chapter 13

The School of Ballet, Warwickshire

Fairy lights traced the edges of the windows of the ballet school, and tealights hung from the surrounding trees, twinkling in the dusk. Lila stepped out of the car, a vintage V8 Pilot, a stole draped around her shoulders, setting off her floor-length ivory gown to perfection, our dad smiling proudly by her side. There was a collective gasp from the wedding guests, as we all walked into the room.

Lila looked beautiful – and it was nothing to do with the dress, or anything she was wearing. After our chat the previous night, her anxieties seemed to have disappeared, replaced with a kind of calm contentment. She was ready.

Her hair, small sections curled and pinned in silver-screen style, suited her perfectly – I knew then I'd been right to

choose Andy as the hairdresser. The actresses on the top costume dramas raved about him. When Lila and I had first
talked about 1920s styling, back in the spring, Andy had
sprung to mind immediately. He might have been pure
TOWIE on the surface, but under that deep spray tan, he had
a comprehensive knowledge of period hairstyles and a way of
making even the most highly strung female feel relaxed.

I focused on my sister – and the look that Ollie was giving
her as he watched her walk towards him up the aisle.

Lila's voice was shaking a little as she said her vows, and I
noticed Ollie give her hand a squeeze. As they kissed, a cheer
went up from the crowd. I glanced back and saw Mum and
Dad on the bench seats behind us. They were next to each
other, and both beaming with pride.

After the ceremony, Lila and her new husband descended
the stone steps, and we showered them with flower petal
confetti.

'She looks very happy,' Mum whispered to me.

'He's a lucky man,' Dad added. There were tears of pride
in his eye.

'He is,' Mum said.

Dad put his arm around Mum and held her close.

Amber and I were just congratulating ourselves on a job well
done, during the speeches, when the room fell quiet and I

saw Ben making his way over to the microphone. My chest went tight. This was not in the plan – my brother, who had been so vague and unpredictable lately – had definitely not been invited to give a speech at the wedding.

Lila hadn't noticed. Her back was to him, and she was gazing into Ollie's eyes, oblivious to whatever it was that was about to unfold.

Ben was clearing his throat. Mum gave me a questioning look, as if I'd organised this without mentioning it to her.

'So, here we all are,' Ben said. Lila's face registered alarm, and she too looked at me, panicked. Of all of us on the top table, Ollie was the only one who remained relaxed, sipping from his glass of Champagne. Ben cleared his throat and began to speak.

'Lila's always got what she wanted –'

I desperately wanted to do something – snatch the mic from him, make it all stop. But he was two guests away from me, and if I moved it would be evident to the whole room that something had gone wrong – and I didn't want to risk that. Not yet. I had no choice but to watch on anxiously.

Lila looked confused, as if she too imagined that I had some greater plan here.

When I'd run through the list of potential hazards for the wedding and embarked on damage-limitation I had failed to think about Ben. I had connected him only with not caring – upsetting Lila by not turning up – so the moment I had received his RSVP I thought we were out of the woods.

'And it seems she set her sights on a nice guy –' His words were slow and considered, dragged out by the wine he'd been drinking – his cheeks were unusually flushed and he had beads of sweat on his forehead, '– this time –,' he continued, to a room that had fallen awkwardly silent.

Please stop, I thought. Please don't say anything more.

'Don't worry,' he said, meeting my eyes. 'I'm not going to embarrass anyone. They're a wonderful couple, and I'm very, very proud of my sister today.'

'Nice speech your brother gave,' Ollie's best man Eliot said to me, his fiancée Gemma by his side. 'I haven't seen that side to him at work,' he added. I couldn't work out if he was being sarcastic, but I felt desperately relieved that my worst fears hadn't played out.

'Let's hope everything goes as smoothly for us, eh Eliot,' Gemma said.

'It can't be long for you guys now,' I said.

'Probably not,' Gemma said. 'We haven't managed to agree on a date yet, or, well – anything else much.'

'She's very hard to please,' Eliot said, laughing.

'I am not,' she said. 'Anyway, can we go out for that smoke now? I'm dying.'

'Old habits,' Eliot said, apologetically. 'I think we must be the only people in the country who still smoke. But it's kind of a romantic thing for us. Gemma works in the bank opposite mine, and that's how we met.'

'Sheltering under the Pret awning as it poured down with rain,' Gemma said, laughing at the memory.

'Yep,' Eliot said. 'I don't think she was immediately convinced I was The One.'

'You persuaded me in the end,' Gemma said. 'Right. Out we go.'

I didn't know Eliot or Gemma well but I'd warmed to them. They were the kind of people you felt at ease around quickly.

The reception all went smoothly. Lila and Ollie had danced their first dance to an admiring crowd of friends and family. Lila hadn't simply danced, she'd glided – and while Ollie wasn't a professional, it hadn't showed, she'd carried him somehow.

The pace had picked up now, and Amber and I were dancing with a few friends to the soul band I'd arranged – it was a relief and a joy to see how popular they were, both with the guests our age, the kids, and our parents' generation.

But I was distracted. After his attempt at a speech, Ben seemed to have disappeared – and while I was unsure of his whereabouts, I had a lingering feeling of uneasiness. There was something weird about the way he was acting, and I couldn't ignore it.

I left the dance floor and went back out into the area where we'd all been seated for the wedding breakfast.

My brother was staring down at his phone in the semi-darkness, the screen lighting his face with a blue-white glow. When he glanced up at me I saw that his eyes – green like mine, like Lila's, were slightly red and bloodshot.

'That was a nice thing you did back there,' I said.

'You sound surprised.'

'I guess I am, a bit,' I said. I hadn't known what was going to come out of my brother's mouth. That's how distant we'd become.

He shrugged, cast his eye back to his phone.

'Put that away for a minute, Ben.'

Out of surprise, more than obedience, he pocketed the phone and looked back at me.

'What's going on with you lately?' I asked.

'Nothing.'

'You were vague about coming today, kept us all guessing, and then . . . I don't get it, Ben.'

'It's nothing.'

I raised an eyebrow.

'OK. It's complicated.'

I thought of the familial bonds that had brought us all together under one roof that day and realised how very fragile they were. I put a hand on my brother's arm and tried to bridge the gap. His gaze was cast down, and I thought for a moment that something in him had softened. Looking at his face, crumpled and weary, I thought of the times at the house when we were young. When he'd trip in the garden, gravel embedding itself in his knees, and I'd pick him back up, hold him close until his sobbing slowly subsided. Back then his heart and skin and soul had felt part of mine, just like Lila's did. I guess I wanted him to feel better, because that was my job. Making things right with him was the only way I could feel OK about being me.

'I think it's time I went home,' Ben said.

When Ben left, in a taxi, I returned to the party, but the buzz of excitement I'd felt earlier had disappeared, replaced with a strange new sadness. The music that had sounded so sweet just half an hour ago now just seemed loud.

'Here you go,' Amber said, passing me a Champagne glass. My heart lifted at the sight of her friendly face, and of the drink. 'Bellini,' she said. 'I think you've earned it.'

'Thanks,' I said. I smiled, but my mind was still reeling. However, one glance across the dance floor to where Lila and Ollie were standing, arms around each other and both laughing, their faces close, confirmed that everything that really mattered today was going OK. I thought of Lila and Ollie's faces when I'd handed over my wedding present to them – the set I'd made of their wedding. I'd worried they might think it was silly, but Lila's eyes had lit up when she saw it.

She and Ollie said it was the perfect way for them to remember the day.

Amber and I danced for a while, and I started to push aside my concerns about Ben. He couldn't ruin today – nothing could – and if he wanted to deal with whatever anger or problems he had on his own, then so be it.

'Cheeseboard's out,' Amber said, nudging me. I was about to follow her over, when I heard my name.

It was his voice. So familiar. Gravelly, but you could always hear a smile in it. Sam. Dressed in a suit and clean-shaven. He looked more mature, in a good way. His hair was close-cropped, with short sideburns, and apart from the dark metal ring high in his ear, the skater boy was all but gone.

'Hi,' I said, my voice barely sounding. Then I remembered my manners. 'Amber, Sam. Sam, Amber.'

'I'll leave you guys to catch up,' Amber said, excusing herself. 'I'm afraid I'm not missing that cheeseboard out of courtesy.'

'Sorry to get here late,' he said. 'There was crazy traffic on the motorway. Your sister looks amazing,' Sam said.

'Doesn't she?' I said, smiling proudly.

'And you don't look so bad yourself,' he said. He smiled, then cast a glance at my bridesmaid's dress. His eyes drifted over the full skirt, the floaty fabric. I felt silly – like a little girl dressed up as a princess for a party.

A flush crept onto my cheeks. He was being polite. This

really wasn't the kind of look he'd ever dug – we both knew that.

We were standing apart from one another, and his posture was awkward. Our friendship and easy way with one another seemed a world away now. My heart felt heavy. He must have felt the same way, as he gave me a hug, slightly rigid and out of sync, but a hug all the same, and it felt good to be close to him again. The trace scent of the coconut hair wax he used that reminded me of summer.

'Great party,' he said. 'Lila told me you're the one responsible for making it all happen.'

'Lila and Ollie had the vision,' I said. 'I just sorted a few of the details.'

'Whatever you say. Do you want to go and get a drink?' Sam said, pointing over at the bar. 'It would be good to chat.'

It would be good to chat. The words lingered as I tried to find a way to reply. *It would be the best thing ever to chat*, I thought. *It would be* incredible *to chat. Chatting to you again is pretty much all I've thought about for the past few months.*

'Sure,' I said.

Chapter 14

Back in London on Sunday evening, with the wedding still fresh in our minds, Amber and I were sitting in our living room, in t-shirts and jeans, drinking tea. Since Lila's wedding the smile had barely left my face – all of the time planning had culminated in an unforgettable day.

Lila and Ollie were off on their honeymoon in Paris, and I was left feeling proud that I'd been part of a day that had meant so much for her and Ollie. And I also felt a warm glow at the memory of talking to Sam again.

'It was AMAZING,' Amber said, lying back on the nest she'd made from sofa cushions. 'From start to finish, definitely the best wedding I've ever been to.'

'The cake was a total hit. I think you probably picked up quite a few future customers, if you're looking.'

Amber smiled. 'Not right now, but maybe one day.'

'Anyway, I'm looking forward to a decent night's sleep

tonight – it'll be the first one I've had since Lila and I started planning.'

'What was up with your brother at the wedding?'

'So you noticed he was acting weird too?'

'Yes, I heard him on the phone at one point,' Amber said, as if she was just recalling it now. 'He seemed upset about something.'

'Probably lost a few quid on the stock exchange. That's all that seems to matter to him these days.'

'No,' Amber said. 'It wasn't that. I don't think it was to do with work. He said they had to make a decision, or he was going.'

'A woman?' I said. Ben hadn't talked about anyone – not for years. I'd started to wonder if maybe city life had turned him celibate.

Amber shrugged. 'I probably shouldn't have said anything, I only caught a few words. But it just seemed odd, at such a happy occasion. I thought it was worth mentioning.'

'Right,' I said. 'Thanks.'

Amber got to her feet and started to tidy the kitchen. I went into my room and got out my phone to call Ben.

There'd been a time when I wouldn't have thought twice about calling him. And yet now – I braced myself for Ben's likely response to my call – guarded, cynical.

The ringtone went on, and in spite of myself I felt a little wave of relief when it switched to answerphone.

'Hey, it's Ben. You've just missed me. Leave me a message and I'll call you right back.'

Tears sprung to my eyes. I hadn't heard his voicemail for a while, so rarely did I call him, but – unlike Ben himself – it hadn't changed. There on that recorded message was the calm, funny and kind man that I'd grown up with.

I was caught out by the beep, and it was a second until I composed myself enough to leave a message. When I did speak the words came out haltingly.

'Ben, hi, it's me. Hazel. I wanted to . . . I guess I just wanted to say. If you . . . I hope you're OK. Anyway, I'm here. If you ever want to talk, I mean. You can call me.'

I hung up before I could make any more of a mess of it. I don't know what I'd really intended to say but it had definitely come out wrong.

Ben wouldn't ring back. I knew that already.

An hour or so later I climbed in bed, pulling the duvet up over me, taking a paperback from my bedside table to read. Everything felt quiet now that the wedding was over.

I was so immersed in my novel, I barely registered my phone buzzing with a new message. I got to the end of my chapter, and picked it up. My heart lifted when I saw there was a new message from Lila. I hadn't expected to hear from her, given that she was on her honeymoon.

Hey Sis. Thank you again! What a day. Having the best
honeymoon ever, too. Oh, by the way can I pass your
email on to Eliot and Gemma? They're interested in
having a chat.
Lila xx

The joy in Lila's voice seemed to come right into the
room with me. She sounded like herself again.

Chapter 15

'So – how was the big day?' Josh said on Monday morning, leaning over the edge of my desk. 'Don't tell me you had all that cake and no leftovers.'

'Nothing,' I said, laughing. 'I'm sorry, Josh. You haven't met my family – they are animals when it comes to baked goods. And Amber's cake was a triumph. Utterly impossible to resist.'

He smiled. 'So – tell me, how did it go? Did all your planning pay off?'

'Spectacularly, if I do say so myself. Have a look at this.' I passed him my iPad, showing the unofficial photos that Amber and I had taken.

Josh swiped his finger over the screen. He nodded, impressed. 'Woah, it looks great,' he said. 'What a brilliant venue. Did your sister and Ollie enjoy themselves?'

'They had the best day of their lives.'

'The place looks fantastic – and her dress is great too. I'll have you know I'm not normally good at saying stuff like that – but that really is a great dress.'

Laughing and talking with Josh again felt good. Things were back to normal between us, with not a trace of the strangeness that had come about when I was worried about Lila.

'Do you think you'll ever do it?' I asked.

He shrugged, and smiled. 'It's complicated.'

'OK, I'll stop prying.'

'There's no big secret,' he said with a shrug. 'Sarah just seems keen one minute, dead against it the next. It's not always easy talking about the future with her.'

'She's better with the present?'

'Yes. She's a free bird. Lives moment to moment.'

'Maybe we could all benefit from being a bit more like that,' I said.

After lunch, I saw there was a personal email in my inbox, alongside the work ones. It was from Eliot, with Gemma CCd in. I opened it, curious.

Hi Hazel,

Great to see you at the wedding. Gemma and I loved what you put together and were so impressed when Ollie told us you'd managed it in a matter of months. We've decided

that we'd like some help getting our day perfect – it's all
relatively last-minute ... hence us needing an extra pair of
hands, but we were wondering if you'd be up for the job?

I felt a burst of excitement as I read the email – they were
offering me work – for money – doing something that for
me was a pleasure.

Keen as I was to do it, I held myself back from pressing
reply. This was someone's wedding day – if I said yes, I had to
follow through properly. I should think about this, over a cup
of tea at least.

As if she'd read my thoughts, an instant message from
Amber popped up in the corner of my screen.

From: Amber
Priority heads up. Muffins in the kitchen. You have two
minutes to get there before the whole office email goes
out. I'll put the kettle on.

I looked over at Amber and she gave me a smile.

I got up and walked over to the kitchen.

Wedding planning. It made such good sense, I don't know
why I hadn't considered it earlier. I'd been enjoying planning
Lila and Ollie's big day – it was really just like decorating
another set. So why shouldn't I look at doing it profession-
ally? So many people in London were money rich, time

poor – but didn't want to compromise on the most important day of their lives. I could help make it easy for them. OK, so there were plenty of people doing it already, who had more experience . . . but perhaps last-minute weddings could be my USP?

'Cinnamon and raisin,' Amber said, as I arrived at the kitchen.

'Yum.' I picked one up and took a bite.

'How's your morning going?' Amber asked, as she poured tea for us both.

'Good, thanks. Just had a bit of a surprising request, as it happens.' I lowered my voice to a whisper. 'Eliot – Ollie's best friend, has just asked if I'll plan his wedding for him,' I said, feeling instinctively that this was something I could share with Amber.

'Interesting,' she said, tilting her head. 'Flattering too. So you're thinking of going into business, on the side?'

'I don't know. I haven't replied.'

'It's only one wedding,' Amber said. 'You could carry on working here, as normal, and just see how it goes.'

I took in the suggestion and mulled it over.

'It's completely doable,' Amber reassured me, sensing my unvoiced doubts. 'Have a chat and see how it all fits. What have you got to lose?'

When I got back to my desk, ten minutes later, a stampede of our colleagues headed into the kitchen as word of the muffins spread. I took the moment of quiet as an opportunity – and tapped out a reply to Eliot saying that I'd love to meet. As I did, my neck prickled with anticipation. I was going to do this. And I was going to do it well.

I met Eliot and Gemma after work the next day, in a café near Liverpool Street. I'd stayed up until the early hours the night before, trawling through the websites of the UK's top wedding planners and seeing how they did it – from contracts to pricing structures. After squinting at the calculator on my phone for what seemed like hours, I'd settled on a rate that seemed right, with a deposit upfront and more to pay after the event. I hoped that Eliot and Gemma would agree.

We greeted each other and sat down at a booth in the corner, away from the loud chatter of the other customers.

'Thanks for coming over to meet us,' Gemma said. She was wearing a bright red dress, and her hair was expensively highlighted. By her side, Eliot looked far more conventional, a pale grey shirt, his dark hair clipped short, with sideburns. He might have been Ollie's best friend, but they were from different worlds – Ollie's the Mac-tapping world of flat whites and sofas, as he wrote screenplays, Eliot the early mornings of life as a trader.

'You too. Take a seat. What can I get you to drink?'

'A coffee, please,' Eliot said.

'Same for me,' Gemma said.

'So – a few formalities to get out of the way first,' I said. 'I hope you are OK with the paperwork and pricing structure I sent over?'

'Oh yes, fine,' Gemma said breezily. 'No probs at all. I'll transfer you the deposit this morning and put the signed copies in the post.'

'Thank you,' I said. Relief swept through me. 'Now, to the interesting bit. I remember that when we spoke, you hadn't quite made your mind up about when you were getting married. Have you reached a decision on that yet?'

'We have. Finally,' Eliot said. 'The thing is, it's—' He glanced at Gemma and smiled, then looked back at me. 'It's going to be soon.'

'This Christmas,' Gemma said. 'And we want it to be big, glitzy and sparkly. No holds barred.'

'We're not doing that badly, actually, Hazel. We've already got a few venues in mind – this is our ideal one.'

Eliot swiped his iPad then passed it to me with the image of a stunning castle taking up most of the screen.

'Mackleford Castle,' Gemma said, proudly. 'Classic, traditional – everything I want this wedding to be. God, I'm all about this place. Look at it, Hazel. It's gorgeous. So romantic. Hidden away up in the Highlands – don't you think it's perfect?'

'I've heard of it,' I said, casting my eye over the images. I remembered making a few phone calls, scouting it out on behalf of the locations department – in the end we'd judged it beautiful but too expensive, and too remote. It was located up in the Scottish Highlands and wasn't an easy place to reach. 'It's lovely.'

'My parents would like it,' Eliot said, taking another look.

'That matters,' Gemma said, in a tone that was only half-playful. 'You don't think it's too expensive, though?' she looked at Eliot.

'I'll be getting a bonus soon. That'll cover it. Don't worry, Gemma – I want to do this.'

'You know I'm not bothered about money,' Gemma said, softly. 'I mean that.'

'I want to pay for somewhere perfect for us to get married,' he insisted. 'Let me do that much.'

Gemma gave a resigned nod and a smile.

'OK,' I said. 'Well, it sounds like you've set your heart on the place. Let's see what we can do.'

Chapter 16

That evening, Amber and I ate our dinner together at the flat. I told her about the meeting with Gemma and Eliot, and my plans for their wedding.

'I seem to have encountered my first setback,' I explained. 'So they already have a very specific venue in mind – and it has to be at Christmas-time. But unfortunately when I called the castle up they're already fully booked – which I'd half expected.'

'Oh no,' Amber said, furrowing her brow.

'That's what I thought, at first,' I said. I brought my iPad up to show her a new image. 'But look at this baby.'

'Castle Belvedere,' Amber read. 'Nestled in the wilds of the Scottish Highlands – an exclusive and unforgettable experience. Wow. That looks incredible.'

'Doesn't it?' I said proudly. 'I knew I'd struck gold, and I called them up right away to discuss availability –

thankfully, perhaps because they are just a little bit remote – they still have a weekend wedding space available before Christmas.'

'That's great news. In another world I'd get married there,' Amber said, dreamily. 'Not that I have anyone to marry right now – but for the sake of a damn good party.'

'The budget they've given me is really generous. I was hoping I might have a bit more cash to work with than I did for Lila and Ollie's wedding – but this is something else. I guess it's just not an issue for them.'

'Can you imagine what that would be like,' Amber said.

'Nope.' I shook my head. 'And I don't expect it to ever be my life – which is what makes all of this such a treat. It's like someone sending you out with their credit card, and telling you to fulfil your wildest dreams. And to commission the best wedding cake baker you know,' I said, with a smile.

Amber narrowed her eyes at me in suspicion. 'Don't tease,' she said.

'I'm not!' I laughed. 'I mean no guarantees – Gemma and Eliot will get the final call, but once they've tasted the cakes you make I can't imagine there's going to be much of a contest.'

'Oh God. That would be amazing,' Amber said, her usually loud voice barely more than a breath. 'You're serious, right?'

'Of course I am.'

'A Christmas wedding,' she said. 'All those delicious spices, ginger, cinnamon, some of my favourite flavours. I can think of one recipe already.'

My phone rang, and a little reluctantly, as I was enjoying the conversation, I got to my feet to answer it.

I checked the screen: Sam.

My heart thudded in my chest when I saw the name. I don't know what I'd expected to happen after we met up again at Lila's wedding, but this had caught me off guard. We were talking again. At the very least.

'I'd better get this,' I said to Amber, excusing myself. I hadn't told her the backstory. As far as she knew, Sam was simply an old friend, nothing more, nothing less. And in a way, that was all that he was.

'Hey, Sam,' I said, nipping into my bedroom quickly and answering the phone as breezily as I could.

'Hi Hazel,' he replied. That laidback, sleepy voice I'd heard so many times, long evenings hanging out at my house or his, days in the park, skating and drinking cheap cider. Then one day that voice had shifted from simply being part of the soundscape of my life to being the sound of everything I wanted.

I settled on the sofa to talk to him. I could hear Amber clattering around, tidying up the dishes after dinner, and was glad that she wouldn't be able to overhear us talking.

'It was good to see you at the wedding,' he said.

I opened my mouth to reply, but no sound came. It had been good. Better than anything. He carried on talking.

'We shouldn't leave it so long next time.'

'You're right,' I said, thankful that my voice seemed to be in working order again.

'In fact that's why I'm calling,' Sam continued. 'I know things got kind of weird . . .'

I held my breath, and silently prayed he'd stop there. I didn't want to talk through all of this, least of all on the phone – the humiliation still felt fresh.

'Anyway, it's simple,' he continued, seemingly thinking better of having the conversation too. 'I don't want to wait another six months before we see each other again, Hazel. I've been meaning to come and see you in London for ages, I've just never quite got around to it. But why don't we make it happen? Next weekend?'

I thought of the things I'd pencilled in to my calendar – a swing dance class, a night at the cinema. They weren't impor-tant. Not really. 'Next weekend would be great.'

'I can stay over, right?' he asked.

'Of course you can. Amber's in the other room now, but there's a sofa. We can go out for a pint locally on Saturday night, then head out to the market on Sunday morning.'

'Sounds great. I'll see you on Saturday in that case,' he said brightly.

I said goodbye, and put down the phone. My heart was thudding hard.

The next day at work, I arrived to an overflowing in-tray. Emma must've worked late the previous night – and work for Emma tended to consist of shifting things from her own desk onto mine. I sipped my coffee and sifted through the documents, working out what was most pressing.

None of it bothered me – nothing was going to kill my buzz today. I had the bubble of a secret inside me. Two in fact. I was meeting my sister at lunchtime to hear all about her honeymoon – I'd got her text late last night:

'We're back! And I can't wait to see you. Picnic in the park at 1?'

And then the other reason. The one I couldn't stop thinking about. The fact that Sam and I were talking again. More than that – he was coming to visit.

'Psst,' I hissed at Josh. He glanced over at me and smiled. I nodded towards the kitchen, and he took out his headphones and came over to my desk.

'Coffee?'

'Yes. You've got five minutes, right?'

'Nothing's that urgent today,' he said. 'Or at least, no more than usual.'

In the kitchen I filled both our mugs, and leaned back against the kitchen counter.

'What's that smile on your face?' Josh asked.

'I had an interesting phonecall last night.'

'Really. How quaint. Who even has phonecalls these days?'

I shrugged. 'It is a bit retro, I guess.'

'So who was it?'

'A friend.'

'Holding your cards close to your chest as ever, then, Hazel.'

'Yes. For now at least. Anyway, how are you and Sarah doing?'

'We're all right. On the rare occasions we're actually together, that is.'

'Where is she now?'

'Spain. Up a mountain somewhere.'

'Any reason?'

'Sarah doesn't need a reason.' There was a slight weariness in his voice when he spoke about her – one I hadn't heard before.

'You OK with that?'

'I have to be OK with it, Haze. I don't want to feel like I'm trapping her. It's just – it's difficult sometimes. We were meant to be seeing my sister's new baby this weekend ... I know Sarah's not that into babies, but this is family and ...'

'And she just went on holiday without warning you?'

I hadn't meant it to sound so judgmental, but it came out that way.

'It's what she does.' His tone was a little defensive.

'I'm sorry. I shouldn't have said that.'

'Don't worry. You're not the first. She says she doesn't want to be tied down,' Josh said. 'But then every so often, after she's had a few drinks . . . she does say maybe more security would help.'

'Right,' I said. 'I don't think I really understand where she's coming from.' Maybe I'd be able to, if Josh was a commitmentphobe, but he'd never struck me as one. 'It all sounds a bit confusing.'

'It is,' Josh said, simply. 'It is. And after all this time together, I haven't come any closer to working out how to handle it. I just wait for the phase to pass, and it usually does.'

I left the office at one, and headed straight over to the green to see Lila. Her rehearsals at Sadler's Wells – which she'd gone straight back into on returning from her honeymoon – were only a short walk away.

I couldn't wait to see her, and to hear how the honeymoon had gone. Not that I wanted ALL the details . . . but it was unusual for us to have a week like this, where no information was shared, where we were in the dark about one another's lives, and I wanted to rectify that.

Last night I'd packed a hamper with sandwiches, grapes and sausage rolls, Bakewell tarts and ginger ale and brought it into work with me. I crossed the green, my iPod earphones in and a soundtrack of rare groove bringing out the golden summery highlights in the late August day. We would fend off autumn for as long as we could.

I laid out a rug under the willow tree that had become our regular place since she moved out and we had begun to need one. A moment later I saw her approaching through the grass, denim dungarees and a white t-shirt on, her long blonde hair in a loose side plait. We hugged hello. I pressed my cheek against hers, wanting to feel, for certain, that she was really her, that she was really back.

'You're doing that thing,' she whispered.

'I am not.'

'You're squeezing my face with your face.' She pulled away and wrinkled her nose, then smiled.

'I missed you, that's all.'

'I missed you too. Probably not as much, but a bit.' She laughed, and so did I. Because it was true. And because that was OK.

'How was it?'

'Incredible,' Lila said, dreamily. She sat back on the rug, and picked off a grape. 'We had a lovely hotel, and spent most of our time there, or schmoozing around art galleries. It was so nice to spend time together without work to think of, and with all of the memories of the wedding still so fresh in our minds. I think it's all I talked about for the first couple of days, at least.'

'Sounds lovely,' I said. There was a pretty glow in her cheeks, and her eyes were bright again.

'Thanks again for everything you did on the wedding. It was amazing. The most perfect day ever.'

'Good,' I said. 'I'm happy to hear you thought that.'

'And I gather you've got more wedding planning to come?'

'Yes,' I said, eager to share the news with her. 'I met with Eliot and Gemma and we talked through their initial ideas for the wedding.'

'Don't tell me – big, lavish, decadent, loud?'

I laughed. 'Yes. And sparkly. Very sparkly.'

'Ooh, nice. I love the idea of a winter wedding.'

'Yes – it'll be completely different from yours, obviously, which will be interesting.'

'Not to mention those two will have quadruple the budget, I'm sure.' She caught herself. 'Not that I'm envious – honest,' she smiled. 'Just stating facts – both Eliot and Gemma are total hotshots in the city, in case they were too modest to mention that.'

'They didn't spell it out, but I got the impression that money wasn't really an object.'

'Brilliant news for you, of course. You'll be able to do whatever you want. Castles, snow machines, the works!'

'Yes. I'm looking forward to it.'

The previous night I'd started work on a set modelled on a room at Castle Belvedere, with snow-dusted decorative branches and fairy lights giving the venue a wintery, but cosy, feel.

'So – what else is new?' Lila asked.

'I got a call last night.'

'Sam,' Lila said, a mischievous grin forming.

I nodded.

'I thought something was going on when you guys were talking at the wedding.'

I shrugged, feeling embarrassed now, sure that I was making a big deal out of something that would most likely turn out to be nothing.

'He's finally figured it out. I knew it!'

'It's not like that. I'm just hoping we can get back to how things were. He's coming to stay this weekend – as a friend, of course.'

'Of course,' Lila said, unconvinced.

'I thought there was a connection at the wedding, when we spoke again. Perhaps this is what we needed, a bit of time and space apart.'

'Maybe he had a bit of growing up to do,' Lila said. 'It's the only excuse, surely, for not being able to see that he should be with you.'

I gave her a nudge. 'Don't. And anyway, stop playing the sage. You've only been married five minutes, you know.'

'Oh God. Am I acting like a know-it-all? I didn't mean to . . . you know I haven't got the first clue about love, apart from knowing that I didn't want to let Ollie go. But you and Sam – any fool can see you two should be together.'

I shook my head. I wasn't sure I was ready to go there again, even in my mind.

'Enough about me. How about you?' I asked. 'Are you feeling OK about everything, I mean what we talked about before the wedding?'

Lila nodded, and I could tell she was steeling herself. 'I'm not going to bury my head in the sand about it. I've been to see my GP. She said we should just try as normal, but she can refer me to a specialist if I want. Ollie's going to come with me.'

'That's good,' I said. 'I hope it goes well.'

She smiled, and gave a resigned little shrug. 'What will be will be, I guess. But Ollie and I are happy together, and that's what matters.'

Chapter 17

I rearranged the photos on my dresser, and tidied the cushions on my bed for the dozenth time – putting the one with the fox design on top. My mind had been buzzing for the last couple of hours. Imagining what it would be like to see Sam again, properly, like this, and hoping that I would be able to hide my feelings somehow.

I checked the clock – 7 p.m. He was due any minute. I felt as if I was a teenager again, as if I'd learned nothing between then and now that would equip me for this ... whatever it was – encounter.

Amber put her head around my bedroom door. 'Still waiting?'

'I'm not waiting,' I said. 'I'm just here, in my home, and my friend's about to arrive. I'm not exactly going to go anywhere, am I?'

'OK, touchy,' Amber said.

She was right, I'd overreacted. I was blowing this whole thing way out of proportion already. 'I'm sorry. What was it you wanted to say?'

'I've thrown together some chilli con carne, and made a massive batch, so I just wondered if you guys wanted to join me.'

Perhaps Sam and I could go out after dinner, instead. 'That would be great,' I said.

The doorbell rang, and my heart jumped a little. I glanced over to the mirror and gave my appearance a final check, then headed downstairs.

'Hey you,' Sam said, as I answered the door. He leaned in and kissed me on the cheek. I hugged him and took in the familiar scent, coconut.

'Come on in,' I said.

He had a sports bag slung over his shoulder, and brought that up with him.

'Do you fancy having dinner here first? I mean, I know you probably want to get out and see some of east London, but Amber's cooked and . . .'

'Eating in would be great. We've got plenty of time to explore.'

'Cool,' I said. I was acting weird, and I couldn't stop it. It felt like the harder I tried to act just like I always had with Sam, the more I ended up stumbling over my words. We went into the flat and Amber was standing in the kitchen.

'Amber, Sam, Sam, Amber,' I said quickly. 'You guys remember each other from Lila's wedding, right?'

'Yeah, I think we met,' Sam said, nonchalant to the point of being slightly off-hand. I looked over at Amber, hoping she wouldn't take it the wrong way.

'Sam!' Amber said. 'Yes, of course we did.' She smiled brightly in welcome, combating his reserved manner with cheer. Good old Amber, I thought. It would take more than a little unfriendliness to dent her positivity.

'I hope you're hungry,' she went on. 'I've made the most enormous vat of chilli, and I'm certainly not going to be able to eat it all myself. Or at least I think I probably shouldn't.'

He looked into the pot curiously, and smiled his appreciation. 'Smells good,' he said.

'Beer?' I asked. They both nodded, and I got three cold Tiger beers from the fridge and cracked them open.

'Your bed for tonight,' I said, pointing over at the sofa.

'Cool,' he said, chucking his bag down on it.

Half an hour later, the three of us were sitting around the kitchen table, and Sam was filling Amber in on some of the old times we'd shared.

'Did I ever mention that she was a brilliant skateboarder?' Sam said.

'No,' Amber said, laughing. 'I had no idea. Hazel – you really are a woman of many talents.'

'Oh, haven't skated for years,' I said, thinking of the battered skateboard that was now gathering dust in the cottage attic. 'But that was how Sam and I got to be friends. There wasn't that much to do in our area, growing up – but what there was was a skate park, and we got chatting there one day.'

'She made a welcome change from all the testosterone,' Sam said, smiling at me.

'Nice that you guys share so much history,' Amber said.

I was relieved that the tension between Sam and Amber that had been there right at the start seemed to have eased now. It had always been a bit weird introducing him to new people; he had a tendency to come across as arrogant, but I knew that deep down it was shyness, and that was just one of the things I really liked about him – that I felt I knew him better than anyone else could.

'So,' I said, finishing my last forkful of chilli and putting the cutlery back on my plate. 'That was delicious, Amber, thank you.'

'Fantastic,' Sam said.

'Thank you. It's always nicer when I have people to cook for.'

'So what's next?' Sam said. 'Shall we all head out?'

All. Of course. Of course we would all head out, I thought to myself. 'Yes,' I said. 'You're free this evening, right, Amber?'

'Yes, sure,' she said, slightly awkwardly, looking to me to confirm that it was OK if she joined us. Of course it was. It was great in fact. Amber and Sam seemed to be getting along well. I had – if I was honest – kind of hoped that Sam and I might get a chance to be alone, to make sure there was no awkward feeling lingering. But we could do that another day, I guess. I pushed the feeling of disappointment aside, and put on a bright expression.

'Great. Shall we go to the canal boat for cocktails?' I suggested.

We found a table on the canal boat deck, and Sam brought over our drinks. The sun was low in the sky now, but it was still warm.

'So did Hazel tell you about her new venture?' Amber asked.

I felt my face grow hot and hoped it didn't show. 'It's not really that.'

'She's already had one request in, to plan someone's wedding.'

'You're moonlighting as a wedding planner now?' Sam said, his eyebrow raised. 'I thought you liked your job, H?'

'I do.' I felt silly and small all of a sudden, as if I was a frivolous teenager who couldn't quite make up her mind. 'I just kind of fell into it, I suppose.'

'Not really,' Amber said. 'You wanted to do it. You could have said no.'

She was right, of course. I just had a feeling he found the whole wedding thing a bit – well, silly. And so I found myself apologising for it.

'She's amazing at it, of course,' Amber said. 'And I'm hoping she'll let me bake the occasional cake. Because I'm definitely getting tired of my day job.'

'Really?' I said. 'I mean of course, I would love to team up with you. But I didn't realise you were bored at work.'

She shrugged. 'It's not forever. I've realised that much now.'

We fell silent for a moment, and my gaze drifted over to the other young people in the bar. Couples, chatting to one another and kissing, hands grasped tightly together as if one of them might fall overboard at any minute. Groups of girls, dressed up with jugs of lethal-looking cocktails between them, clearly just starting out their night. Their male counterparts in shirts and jeans, talking loudly over pints, knocking each other on the arm for show. Every set-up seemed more, well, normal than ours.

'So, Amber – where are you from, originally?' Sam asked. 'It can't be anywhere as small and boring as our village, that's for sure.'

I smiled, thinking of the close parallels between our hometowns, that we'd found while talking.

'Oh, you'd be surprised . . .' she said, laughing.

'Go on, tell me.' As she spoke, Sam seemed hooked on her every word. It was so obvious, now that I'd spotted it. Sam was enraptured.

The hope that I'd had, that Sam and I might get closer this weekend, disappeared in that moment.

Chapter 18

from: Josh Sanderson
So. Spill.
How was it?

I glanced over to Josh's desk and caught his eye briefly. Emma had had her office door closed all morning, staving off a hangover that was even worse than usual, with a steady supply of coffee from me.

I looked again at Josh's message and my fingers hovered over the keyboard. Part of me wanted to be light and breezy – gloss over the deep disappointment I felt and pretend that everything had gone fine. But I knew Josh would see straight through me.

Not quite how I expected.
Hmm. In a good way?

It wasn't good. That much I knew. Sam had been so caught up in talking to Amber that I'd barely got to talk to him at all – and that certainly hadn't been in my plan. I felt embarrassed even thinking about it, how wrong I'd got everything. Sam must have liked Amber when he met her at the wedding. And I'd been dumb enough to think he'd wanted to come and see me.

Bad way

I typed.

Pretty sure he fancies Amber.

Josh paused, before typing back:

Oh, that's crap.

His message conjured up the smallest of smiles. Earlier that morning I didn't think I'd be able to summon a smile ever again. I'd said goodbye to Sam the previous day, Sunday, and felt sure that he was half looking over my shoulder at Amber. Through the whole weekend it had seemed as if Amber was spotlit in gold light, and I was standing off-stage in the shadows.

I swallowed down my jealousy – it was stupid. It certainly

wasn't Amber's fault that Sam had taken a shine to her. That didn't stop it from hurting, though. Another message pinged through from Josh.

Well, whoever he is, he's not good enough for you

When I got back to the flat that evening, I realised there was only one way to deal with the situation – and that was to embrace it. I wanted Sam to be happy, didn't I? And I wanted the same for Amber. So what if this situation wasn't quite what I'd envisioned. It seemed selfish to deny them both the chance of being happy together.

I texted Sam.

Hi. Great to see you. I thought you might like Amber's number, so I'm sending it over. You should call her. H

I didn't get a reply, and I settled down to work at one of my sets. An hour later I heard laughter from Amber's room. It went on for what seemed like for ever, but must only have been about twenty minutes.

A knock came on my door a few moments after things went quiet.

Amber looked flushed, and had an irrepressible grin on her face. 'Your friend Sam just called.'

'Did he ask you out?'

She nodded. 'He said you were OK with it.'

'Of course,' I said. 'Did you say yes?'

'Yeah. We're going out next weekend.'

'Cool,' I said, feeling deflated but fighting it back.

'Listen, Hazel. You'd tell me if you weren't OK with this, right?'

Amber was so genuine and so sweet about it, that it made the whole situation almost bearable.

'How could I not be?' I said. 'You're great. Sam's great. This is excellent news.'

Chapter 19

The next day, I met with Gemma and Eliot, and was grateful for the distraction.

'Hi, Hazel,' Gemma said, giving me a kiss on the cheek.

'Hey there,' I said. 'I've got us a table out on the terrace, come through – and we can talk everything through there.'

We walked through the café and out onto the decked terrace. The sky overhead was a clear blue, the kind that makes anything and everything seem possible. I ordered coffees for us and brought out a folder I'd set up for Eliot and Gemma's wedding.

'OK,' I said, once we were all sitting down. 'So, I'm really sorry about this, but while I did all I could, I'm afraid I couldn't get you your first choice of venue.'

Gemma's face fell, and she bit her lip. Eliot put his arm around her. 'Sorry. I mean it's stupid to be upset, I shouldn't have set my heart on it – we both know it's late notice. But it just looked so perfect.'

'I know,' I said. 'And I know it must be disappointing for you. But the good news – and there is good news – is that I think I might have found somewhere just as good, and they do have availability.'

Gemma looked sceptical, but there seemed to be an air of cautious optimism with Eliot, at least. 'Shall we take a look, hon? We agreed, didn't we, that if we were going to do the wedding this year then we'd need to keep our options open.'

Gemma nodded, and straightened in her seat. 'Yes. I know you're right. Do you have any pictures?'

I passed her the iPad with the castle's website loaded.

The couple were silent for a moment, scrolling through the images.

Then Gemma looked at Eliot.

My chest felt tight as I waited for their reaction. I knew how slim the pickings were – they really had to like this.

A smile formed on Eliot's mouth, then on Gemma's.

'I think you've found a gem here, Hazel,' Gemma said. 'It's absolutely perfect.'

That evening, Lila and I met in a tapas bar on Exmouth market. I challenged her to a game of table football and took our beers over to the front of the bar. As we played (and she, rather impressively, kicked my butt), I told her how things had panned out with Amber and Sam.

Her face creased up into a frown, and she stood up straight from the foosball table.

'Well, what the hell did you do that for?' Lila said, her voice uncharacteristically harsh.

'What,' I said. 'I didn't do anything ... not really. It was clear that he liked her, and all I did was pass on her details.'

'Clear how?'

'He asked her to join us, laughed at everything she said ... you know. It was obvious,' I said, recalling that night.

'There could have been a hundred other reasons for that. He was probably just being polite. Now you've practically matchmade them.'

'He didn't have to ask her out,' I said.

'Of course not, but he might well have read your message as a nudge to,' Lila said. 'Hazel. You can be really blind to this stuff sometimes.'

I stiffened defensively. 'I'm not being blind. I can just see when two people are right for each other.'

'If you say so,' Lila said, looking away.

'I mean it.'

'You're scared,' Lila said. 'Of really feeling something. That's what I think.'

'So what if I am?' I said. 'Because I really felt something last year, and look how that turned out, Lila – I told Sam, and it resulted in nothing but me losing my best friend, and feeling like an idiot. I'm not prepared to do that again. And anyway – it's too late now.'

'Sorry,' Lila said, backing down at last. 'I shouldn't have interfered.'

'Exactly,' I snapped back. 'Trust me on this. I know I did the right thing.'

Arguing with Lila always upset me. It helped a little, at work the next day, to see that I wasn't the only one feeling rough around the edges. Josh had dark circles under his eyes, and the shadow of stubble on his jaw, a marked difference to how clean-shaven he usually was. 'You all right?'

'Oh, I'm fine,' he said. 'Just didn't sleep much last night.'

'How come, what happened?'

'Nothing. I mean, nothing out of the ordinary.'

I hazarded a guess. 'Sarah?'

'She came back from Spain with a lot of ideas about the way things should be between us. Wanted to talk late about it.'

'Right.'

'She thinks we're growing apart,' Josh said quietly. 'When we should be growing together. She spoke to a shamen about it, apparently.'

'And what does she want you to do?'

'She wants us to go to India together. Or get married. Or build a house in the country together. I don't know,' Josh said, rubbing his temples. 'I feel like it keeps changing.'

'That does sound a bit confusing,' I said. It sounded mad, and infuriating, actually, but I tried to remain diplomatic.

'It is. I sometimes feel like I can't get anything right. But I know relationships need work. So I guess I just have to keep working at this.'

I didn't like seeing Josh upset. I didn't like it at all. Josh, who only ever sought ways to make other people happier. My instinct was to put my arms around him and hug him. But, hard as it was, I fought the urge back.

Chapter 20

The good thing about Amber and Sam getting together, and the dark, wet autumn nights putting the kibosh on the rest of my social life, was that I had plenty of time on my own in the flat – just when I needed it. Being alone in the flat more often meant fewer distractions, and that was what I needed right now. After their first date, I'd distanced myself a little from them. It was the only way I had to feel like less of an idiot, and to get a bit of control back. It had helped me to move on, I guess. She insisted they were only dating, and it was nothing serious, but the fact remained that Sam was part of Amber's life now, not mine.

Once I'd accepted that, things got better. Amber and I had fallen back into our easy way of being, and baking, and eating. And, like I say, they were usually out, so at least I didn't have to see them together.

If I was really going to make a go of wedding planning –

and I was feeling more and more serious about the idea – then I had a lot to learn. Flicking between Pinterest and recipe sites, I could almost nudge it out of my mind – that nagging feeling that Amber and Sam were out together, and I was here on my own.

I didn't need to ask Amber how things were going with Sam – that glow in her cheeks was pretty unmistakable. I was happy for her – she deserved it. And I guess I hoped that it might rub off on me somehow.

I'd spent the time trawling blogs and specialist wedding sites, drawing together images until I had a complete mood-board for Gemma and Eliot's wedding that I knew they were going to absolutely love. There was a pleasant addictive quality to the work of wedding planning – ticking boxes of my to-do list without a boss breathing down my neck and giving me more admin each time I finished something. And – well, there was something nice about dealing with other people's relationships. They always seemed so much more straightforward than my own.

So, now was the time to regroup, and focus on making the most of the opportunity I'd been given. It was the end of September, and in wedding terms, Eliot and Gemma's wedding was getting crazily close. There was still a lot to do.

I'd enjoyed talking with them about their ideas, which were slowly coming into a kind of harmony. Yes, it was Gemma who was leading the more extravagant plans, the requests for husky rides and sleighs, and a snow-covered pine at the entrance to the castle, and Eliot was still reining her in, but their ideas about guests, music, and food were all falling beautifully into line after a few gentle nudges from me. Things were spilling a little outside of the first budget we'd discussed, but from what Lila had said, I got the sense that it didn't really matter. These two inhabited a different world from the one that Lila and I knew, one where Champagne flowed like water, and bills weren't anything to worry about.

With 'Last Christmas' playing in the background to conjure up a festive mood, I worked up some images of table decorations to show to them at our meeting – silvered pine cones and red berries and candle holders that would project the light in the shape of winter branches, to fall across the guests' plates. There was a larger projector I'd seen that would cast a similar shadow on the aisle while the couple walked up it – I was confident Gemma would love it, so had gone ahead and booked it for the day.

Aside from the main cake, Amber had come up with another idea for a display on the side – a trio of small gingerbread houses, dusted with icing sugar. I felt a buzz of excitement as I worked – I knew I could make this the perfect day to take Eliot and Gemma into married life.

I thought of the frustration I'd been feeling at work lately – and then of the money that Eliot and Gemma were offering me.

There was a way out I was starting to see. The germ of an idea began to grow: I wanted to expand, start up a proper business. One compromise at Twenty-One had led to another, until I'd lost sight of what might really make me happy. I had to change things.

But that didn't mean I had to be hasty about it. Emma barely seemed to notice what I did these days anyway. I'd simply have to keep things ticking over, and maintain a low profile. Any spare time, I'd put into my new business – my future.

Later that evening, I was sitting in the living room with Amber. I'd hesitated at first over whether to tell her about my new plan, but decided I couldn't keep it to myself any more. I was too excited.

Her face lit up as I outlined my idea. 'It sounds great.'

'Do you think?' I said. 'You reckon it's OK to stay in the job, for the time being, while I get myself set up?'

'Of course. And you don't owe Emma a thing, so don't worry about that. I think you're really brave.'

'Thank you. I guess I'm just ready for a new challenge,' I said. 'I thought at first that might be the promotion, but now I feel like maybe I get the same buzz from wedding planning. And provided I get it right, there could be good money in it.' My mind was racing with ideas for future weddings. 'Oh, and Amber – it goes without saying that you're welcome to join. Not that I really AM anything yet, but what I am I'd love for you to be part of too. If that makes any sense.' I laughed.

In terms of wedding-cake bakers, I knew I wasn't going to find anyone better.

'I mean, you know I'd like to,' Amber said, biting her lip. 'I can't think of anything more exciting, really, than this, going into business together. But . . .'

'What? You could still keep your day job, like I'm doing. The weddings will probably be on weekends, and even if they aren't you'd have the evenings to bake. You're doing that already.'

A smile began to creep onto her lips, and slowly took over – lighting up her face. 'I think I just ran out of reasons to say anything but a big yes.'

'Great,' I said. 'Let's drink to that.'

As we brought our glasses together, I felt more alive than I had in a long time.

Chapter 21

The next morning, I finished the to-do list I had from Emma, who hadn't arrived in to the office yet, then got out my wedding planning folder. I spent an hour at work researching caterers for Gemma and Eliot's wedding, and drew up a short-list to show them. One had a London branch, so it looked like we'd be able to sample the food without heading up to the Highlands to do it. OK, so that luxury came at a premium, but I was fairly sure that their budget had a bit of give in it.

Emma came in at just after ten. 'You couldn't nip out and get me a bacon and egg baguette, could you, Haze?' she whispered. 'And a strong Americano?'

How it was that she could walk right past the café down-stairs and still need me to run her errands was something I still hadn't figured out.

But, for the first time in weeks, I didn't mind doing it. 'OK,' I said, getting to my feet.

I waited in the familiar coffee queue, my thoughts running over the plan of the day for Gemma and Eliot's wedding. Gemma was keen to have a Ceilidh – that would be next on my list of things to sort out. Perhaps I could tackle that one over lunch.

I got back to the office, and went over to Emma's desk, putting her coffee and sandwich down. 'Here you go,' I said.

'Thanks.'

I was turning go, when she called me back.

'Oh, Haze. Everything sorted for *Christmas at the Manor* now?' she asked.

'Yes. All done.'

'Good. Because there's a progress meeting later. I'll tell them how on top of it all we are. How good you've been at chasing up the bits and pieces we needed to fulfil my vision.'

'Thanks,' I said. Then what she'd said started to sink in. 'Your vision?' I queried, confused. The designs had all been mine. Every single one.

'I mean, I know I've been a bit less hands-on with this project,' Emma said. 'What with everything else that's been going on. But we're a team, aren't we? And you always seem to know *instinctively* just what it is I'm picturing.'

'But Emma,' I said, my voice low and quiet. 'This was my project. From the very start. That's what we agreed.'

'Listen, Hazel. They're on my case,' Emma said, even more quietly. 'Help a girl out, will you?' Then her voice turned

170

light again, almost sing-song. 'I'll explain to Aaron and the others that I've let you take the credit up till now, but it's only fair that I give them the full picture. I've been working hard on the designs for months. Why else would I have spent so much time in my office with the door closed, eh?' Emma gave me a wink.

This wasn't happening. It couldn't be. This was bad even by Emma's standards.

'No way. You can't do that.' The words and emotion that I'd been repressing for months was coming out, whether I wanted it to or not. 'That's not fair. I've worked hard on this project.'

'I can't, can I?' Emma said, her eyebrows raised.

'Look. I put up with you standing in the way of my promotion. But not even letting me have recognition for the work I've already done . . .'

'Oh. This work, do you mean?' Emma said, holding up a sheet of paper.

As I caught sight of it, my cheeks grew hot. It was a contract. The contract I'd signed with Gemma and Eliot. I had left it out on my desk.

'Because this looks rather a lot like moonlighting, if you ask me.' There was a bitter edge to her voice. 'And coupled with this—' she held up the list of caterers I'd put together. 'It's looking more and more like you are taking advantage – using company resources and time for your other . . . venture.'

My chest felt tight. There was nothing I could say to make this go away. It wasn't right. I could try and plead my case to Aaron. But Emma had a point. I'd done enough wrong to make it easy for her to discredit me.

I felt as if I'd hit a dead end.

There was no way I was going to let her hold me to ransom, keep my head down and let her continue to take credit for the work I was doing. There were a thousand truths I could tell the directors about her work over the past months, but I wasn't going to play her game. I wanted to keep my dignity.

'You're right, I should have been honest about the other work. And now I will be. I'd like to give in my notice.'

'That wasn't what I meant,' Emma blundered. 'You don't have to leave, Haze ... I was just saying ...'

'I want to leave. I'll give you a formal resignation letter today.'

'You can't leave ...' she said, desperation in her eyes.

My resolve strengthened.

'Oh – I'm pretty sure I can.'

With that, I turned and went back to my own desk, trying to block out the voice that told me I'd just done something completely mad.

That weekend, reality hit. I'd left my job at Twenty-One, and after working out my notice I'd be unemployed. The wedding planning – which had seemed like such an enticing sideline, was now going to have to be a fully-functioning business, that I could rely on to pay my rent and bills. I paced the flat. I had researched other successful wedding planners a lot over the past few weeks, and picked up tips on growing and building a business – but it would all take time. I had the deposit from Gemma and Eliot, but that would only take me so far. I was going to need more money before their next payment was due. I knew the answer already – I just wasn't ready to accept it yet. I was going to have to call on the bank of Mum and Dad.

I called Dad and told him that I was taking a leap into the unknown, and I could do with a financial lifeboat.

'I'm so proud of what you're doing, Hazel,' he said.

'Thanks,' I said.

'I'll talk to Mum about it, but I have a bit put aside and I'm more than happy to support you while you get on your feet. I've no doubt you'll be able to pay me back soon. Perhaps if I'd had the courage to do something like this, years ago, things might be different now.'

'What do you mean?'

'Well, we both know that a desk job was never my dream. Here's hoping I can live a little by watching you make a better go of it.'

That was it – I couldn't let him down.

Chapter 22

I had a month left to work at Twenty-One, and in a way I was glad. I was in no hurry to leave the people – my boss aside – and everyone was really kind about how much they didn't want me to go. Josh insisted that everyone could see through Emma – that he could sort things out for me – but by then I'd made my decision. I was ready for a clean break and now, particularly with my parents' support, I was actively looking forward to focusing on starting up as a wedding planner.

And even though I was fitting the work into my evening hours, it was all going well. That is, it had been – up until now.

I squinted at the figures on the spreadsheet for Gemma and Eliot's wedding that was open in front of me. I checked my emails and tweaked some of the estimated costs, but something was still wrong. The figures in the two columns were a long way from matching, and the difference from their original budget was far greater than I'd thought. I must have missed something.

I took a sip of coffee, hoping it might jolt my mind into action. It was eleven in the evening, and I had a breakfast catch-up with Gemma and Eliot the next day – I had to figure out what was going on before then.

With some tough negotiating, Belvedere Castle had actually come in under budget – they seemed to realise they weren't likely to get another wedding booking at this late notice. The caterers had given us a great deal – considering the quality of the food, that was. I recalled the hors d'oeuvres they'd given us to try last weekend – miniature Yorkshire puddings and smoked salmon blinis to make your mouth water. Eliot and Gemma had seemed to enjoy it and they'd been happy to delegate the decision to me. I looked back over the agreement with them, and then referred to Eliot's original email. Cogs whirred in my mind and my mouth dropped open. Oh. God.

Carried away with excitement at booking the caterers – the very top of their game – I'd failed to notice that Eliot and Gemma's budget for catering was minuscule. I remembered my conversation with Gemma now, at the start of the project. 'We're not foodies, us. Give us a bottle of wine, good music and entertaining company and we're happy – I don't see the point in splashing half the budget on food people are probably going to be too drunk to really appreciate anyway.' I'd already paid the caterers a deposit, so there was no backing out. When I met Gemma and Eliot tomorrow, I'd just have to explain.

'Two macchiatos and a cappuccino, please,' Eliot said to the waiter at a café near to his work. 'Thanks for coming in so early, Hazel. Really appreciate it. I have an eight-thirty meeting today.'

'No problem,' I said, breezily. I didn't mention that it also suited me pretty well, given I was still officially working another job. I reached down into my bag and got out the wedding folder.

Gemma clapped her hands together excitedly. 'Yay! I just can't wait to see what you've been up to. I know it's going to be amazing.'

I had devoted the small hours of the morning to printing out some of the most stunning images of floral arrangements and table decorations that Pinterest had to offer.

I spread them across the table and Gemma cooed over them, putting her hand on top of Eliot's. 'Aren't these wonderful, darling?'

'Great,' he said. 'Yep. Flowers. All good.'

They spent a few minutes talking over the details for buttonholes and bouquets, until I saw that Eliot's eyes had glazed over a little.

I took a deep breath. OK, I'd smoothed the way, now it was time to come clean. 'Do you remember that amazing catering tasting we went to?'

Eliot nodded. 'Yes. That all seemed fine.' I noticed that he was discreetly checking the time on the clock behind me.

'Yes, they were good, weren't they?' Gemma said. 'I mean, like I said, Hazel. We're more into the spectacle and party aspects of the day, but those caterers seemed fine, and if it fits the budget we're happy. That's sorted already, anyway, isn't it? I'm sure we saw an invoice for the deposit.'

'Yes,' she said. 'You know the figure you gave me. What that absolutely, definitely set in stone?'

Gemma shrugged and looked at Eliot, who nodded his head firmly.

'Right,' I said. Maybe there was still time for me to do something. Make a saving elsewhere. 'It's just . . .'

Eliot checked his mobile.

'Look, I'm so sorry about this,' he said. 'But I'm going to have to run. Can I leave you two to sort out the details?' He gave Gemma a kiss on the top of her head. 'You can fill me in at home, can't you?'

'Sure, love,' Gemma said. 'Leave us to it.'

At home that evening, the conversation with Gemma and Eliot was still running through my head. There seemed to be nowhere obvious to cut back, and whichever way I looked at it, the budget wasn't going to cover the wedding that I'd promised them.

I sat down at the kitchen table.

'Hey you,' Amber said, brightly, when she emerged from her room. 'How's the planning going?'

I let out a groan.

'Something gone pear-shaped?'

'Perhaps. A tiny bit.'

'Put the kettle on and tell me all about it.'

I got to my feet and took out a couple of mugs. 'Sometimes, Amber, you know just the right thing to say.'

She pulled out a chair and sat beside me. I opened up the spreadsheet and Amber read it over my shoulder. 'OK,' Amber said. 'I can see what you mean. It's not looking great. You're going to have to come clean. Honesty is the best policy in a situation like this.'

'You think I could just tell them?'

'Absolutely. And soon. You just spoke with them, right? Why don't you follow up with a phone call, and say there's something else you need to discuss.'

I bit my lip.

'Oh go on, you've coped with Emma all this time. I'm sure you can handle this.'

'Maybe.'

Amber finished her tea quickly. 'I've got to head out, I'm

meeting Sam in half an hour.' She checked the time on her phone. 'But you'll be fine, Hazel,' she said, giving my arm a squeeze. 'You can work this one out, no problem.'

'Thanks.'

Amber left, and I picked up my mobile. I brought up Gemma's number.

'Hi Gemma. Have you got a minute?'

'Sure. I'm just having my nails done, but fire away.'

'There was something I should have told you this morning . . .'

After talking to Gemma I felt as if a weight had been lifted. After all of the worry, she had been surprisingly accommodating about getting the additional funds. She'd said she'd speak to Eliot that evening about it.

The next day, I went to work as usual and treated myself to noodles for lunch. Over my bowl of ramen, I noticed a familiar figure come into the restaurant and sit down at a corner table. He picked up the menu and looked over it, but his eyes were blank. It took me a second to register who it was.

'Hey Eliot,' I called out.

'Hi,' he said, with a weak smile.

'You OK?'

'Yes, fine.' He put a hand to his forehead. 'Well, I've been better actually.'

'What's up?'

'Do you want to join me?' he asked, motioning to the seat opposite him.

'Sure. Has something happened?'

'You could say that.' He put a hand through his hair. 'God. It's been a bloody awful week, Hazel. I probably shouldn't be telling you this, you're going to regret asking me . . .' He gave a wry smile.

'Not at all. Go on.'

'They're making redundancies at RCB and I found out my job's at risk. Nothing's certain but I have a gut feeling that I'm going to be one of the people they let go.'

'I'm so sorry to hear that,' I said. I thought of Ben, who worked at the same firm.

'It's a massive shock. I think I'm still taking it in.'

I nodded. 'Of course. I'm sorry to ask, given what's happened to you – but I don't suppose you know if my brother's job is safe?'

'Oh, Ben'll be fine,' Eliot said, with a trace of cynicism. 'No danger at all of them letting him go.'

'Right,' I said, my relief tempered by slight confusion at the tone in Eliot's voice.

'You won't tell Gemma, will you? About this? I just want to wait until it's certain. I don't want her worrying unnecessarily.'

'I won't say a word,' I reassured him.

'Good, because you know ... I don't know how she would take this. I don't want her to see me differently.'

I paused, then asked the question I couldn't avoid any longer. 'Do you think this is going to affect the wedding?'

'The honest answer is I don't know. It's not long till Christmas. And the costs of the wedding just seem to be mounting up.'

I felt a pang of guilt as he said that. 'I'm sorry ...' I said. 'I should have budgeted better ... I just assumed that money wasn't that much of a consideration for the two of you. That was stupid of me.'

'No –' he said. 'We gave you every reason to think that. And I'm determined to pay for at least half of it, hopefully more – Gemma's been carrying me for too long.'

'What do you mean?' I asked.

'I feel embarrassed admitting it, but Gemma's been paying the lion's share of everything for years – the flat, our holidays. I do what I can, but her salary is almost twice what mine is,' his cheeks coloured as he said it.

'I don't see how she'll be able to respect me at all – now this has happened.'

Chapter 23

That night I got a call from an unlisted number.

'Hazel. Can we talk?'

I'd thought for a moment the male voice was Dad's. That pretty much covered the men who had permission to call me in the middle of the night.

'I know you don't owe me anything,' he said. 'And I'm pretty bloody sure I'd say no if I were you. But I don't know who else to ask.'

It was Ben. And he sounded just pathetic enough for me to say yes.

Ben arrived half an hour later, with a black eye. The kind that's only just started to form, so the skin is tinged red – with the promise of yellow and green and that nasty dark ring that would appear the next day. His hair was a mess.

'Stop staring and let me in, will you,' he said. Then – taking note of the glare I was giving him – he seemed to remember his place. 'Please, Hazel? God knows, today's been bad enough.'

I stood aside and Ben walked past me into the flat. He had lost his characteristic swagger, and as he strode into the room he seemed smaller somehow, a hunch in his shoulders. He walked over to the sofa and sat down, then lowered his forehead into one hand, shielding his face from view.

'Tea?' I offered, in lieu of any better course of action.

'Anything stronger?' He looked up at me and I saw that his eyes were not only bearing the mark of some physical encounter, but were also red-rimmed and bleary, as if he had not slept well for some time.

'I could do you a whisky,' I said, and he nodded. I got out the bottle I'd been given by a supplier at work. I wasn't much of a whisky drinker, so it was still practically full. I poured him one, and – accepting that I was going to need something to get me through whatever it was that was about to unfold – poured a shot over ice for myself.

I passed him the glass, and he emitted a noise that could have been a grunt of gratitude. It was difficult to tell for sure, with his face so creased and weary. I took a large sip from my drink.

'So. Are you going to sit here in my living room in silence, or are you going to tell me what's going on?'

The grunt came again, and then the return to quiet. I began to question why I was even attempting to draw his story out. Ben might have been family but a thought nagged – would he do the same for me? Had he ever done anything that immediately benefited anyone but himself? He had, I reminded myself. Various times. Just not lately.

I couldn't look away from him, though. I couldn't just stop trying with him – he might sometimes act like he wasn't really part of our family any more, but when he was silent I could see the cheekbones that were Mum's, the jawline that was Dad's, and the eyes that would forever link him to me and Lila.

When I saw that, my irritation lifted. If I wasn't here for him, who would be?

I reached out and touched his arm. He flinched, just slightly, but he didn't pull away.

I softened my voice. 'You can tell me, you know, Ben. And unless you've suddenly lost all spatial awareness, it looks a lot like someone's punched you in the face, so we might as well start there.'

Ben took a sip of whisky and then raised his eyes to meet mine.

'It's a total disaster, Hazel. And this time – and believe me, I've tried – I've got no one to blame but myself. I've really messed up.'

'What happened?'

'This,' he touched the fragile skin around his eye, and I could see by the way he winced that it hurt him, 'is what I deserved. In fact I deserved a lot more than this really, I got off lightly.'

'Who did it?'

'Her husband. Although if Eliot had done it I wouldn't have blamed him.'

'What?' I said, trying to piece the information together.

'I should start at the beginning, I guess. I've been sleeping with my boss. Carly Grey. One of the most important women in the city. I had her in the palm of my hand, every time we were together. It's how I got the job, and well, I'm starting to realise now that it's how I've kept the job.'

He paused, his hand returning to the bone of his eye socket, unconsciously touching again the part of his face where his pain showed through.

'So it's been going on since you joined?'

'Yes, two years now. It was exciting at first – and work was going so well. Then my performance started to dip, and well . . . this stuff happens, but I was the only one not getting pulled up on it. I was able to keep on underperforming and she never said a thing to me.'

'Come on, Ben. You can't blame it all on somebody else.'

'I'm not,' he said bluntly. 'I know I'm the one who messed up. And her husband decking me – that I can handle. But not what happened to Eliot. She ended up pinning my mistakes on him, so that they wouldn't have to let me go.'

My heart leapt in my chest as I put the facts together.

'I really did think I was in love with her, Hazel. This is just so bloody humiliating. I'm out of a job, unceremoniously fired after word got out, and everyone in the company knows exactly why.'

'What about Carly?'

'She keeps calling, she came round the flat . . . It's totally weird. All this time I've wanted her to leave her husband for me . . . But now? God, Hazel. I don't want her to do that. I don't want to wreck her family – I don't even feel confident any more that we could make it work if she did.'

'Right. It sounds like you need time to think all this through.'

He nodded. 'I guess. Every time I see her, though – or hear her voice. This sounds pathetic, doesn't it?' he said. His eyes looked even more sorrowful now. 'I want to be with her so badly, but at the same time I know now, that it's not right. It was all a dream, really – and I suppose it boosted my ego believing I could really be that good at my job. Now it feels like everything's falling down around me, and I don't know how to stop it. I don't feel strong enough to push her away.'

Ben told his story, and I just sat and listened. It was the most I'd heard him talk in years. I couldn't fix the pain and humiliation he was experiencing, and I didn't even want to. He needed to feel this, I realised. He needed to hit rock bottom – he'd been crying out to feel this. What I could do, though, was help him find his way back up.

'Do you want to stay here for a few days?' I asked.

He shook his head. 'No, it's fine. I need to go back to my flat and get looking for a new job . . .'

'Come on, Ben.'

'Maybe just tonight,' he conceded reluctantly.

By midnight we had made serious inroads into the bottle of whisky, and somehow my brother and I were laughing like we never had before.

'You two,' Ben said. 'You were always the special ones. Even before Lila got ill and became all that Mum and Dad ever thought about.'

'Sorry, that came out all wrong,' Ben said. 'You see what I mean?' He furrowed his brow and I couldn't help but feel the tiniest bit sorry for him. 'I'm making things even worse. What I was trying to say, is that I was always a bit jealous of you two and your relationship with Mum and Dad.'

'That's really how you feel?' His words genuinely surprised me and emotion welled up. I had read everything so wrong. An idea came to me.

'How would you feel about going back home for a while?'

'No – no way.' He shook his head.

'Think about it. At least think about it.'

Chapter 24

After Ben left, I went to meet Gemma at her and Eliot's flat, near Spitalfields Market.

Gemma opened the door to me in a dressing gown, her cheeks streaked with dark make-up and blotchy from crying. She looked even worse than she'd sounded on the phone.

'He's bottled it,' Gemma said.

I drew in my breath. So it was worse than I'd thought.

'Eliot doesn't want to marry me after all.'

This didn't seem right, though. Eliot had been distressed when we'd talked about his redundancy, yes – but he hadn't mentioned anything about calling off the wedding.

'Come in – see for yourself, he's started packing up his things, he stayed at Lila and Ollie's last night and he's even talking about moving back in with his parents.'

I surveyed the living room of their flat – sleek and stylish, with a few stand-out antiques and a large silver-framed mirror above the mantelpiece. Beyond it I could see the corridor, two suitcases half-filled with clothes, others laying round about.

'He took enough for a few nights, then left it like this, said he'd come back and get the rest later.' She sat down on the sofa and lowered her head into her hands. 'Hazel. What the hell is going on here? I thought we were in love. I've asked him if there's someone else, and he's said there isn't . . . but why else . . .?' She started to sob, then brushed her eyes roughly and stopped.

She looked at me, her eyes wide, searching my face for the answer. 'Did he give you any indication?'

'No,' I said, shaking my head. I felt torn.

'Maybe he never really wanted to marry me at all,' she said. 'That's the only reasonable explanation. But Hazel – I can't believe it. Because I know what love feels like, and this is it. It can't just vanish overnight, can it?'

How was this happening? They couldn't just break up.

'He still loves you,' I said, certain, at least, of that. 'That much I know.'

That night, I called home and asked to speak to Ben.

'Hey,' he said, sounding downbeat.

'You made it back, then?'

'Yes. Mum and Dad have taken me in, tail between my legs and all that.'

'Good.'

'Have you heard from Eliot?' he asked.

'That's partly why I'm calling. He seems to have taken this all really badly – worse than I thought at first. He's left Gemma.'

'Are you serious? Oh, God . . . This is bad. I called them, you know. I spoke to HR – I couldn't quite face speaking to Carly. Told them the whole truth, and that they should give him his job back.'

'And . . .?'

'They said it was more complicated than that. His exit was listed as redundancy and that couldn't just be undone.'

'Oh,' I said, my heart sinking.

'Eliot's a decent guy – he didn't do anything wrong, and he shouldn't be the one losing out in all this.'

'I couldn't agree more. It was horrible seeing Gemma like that, and not even being able to tell her the truth, Ben. Eliot was so ashamed about losing his job he swore me to secrecy.'

'That's hard,' he said. 'So I guess one way or another I've put a spanner in the works with your new business too.'

'Well, yes, you could say that,' I admitted.

'I'm so sorry, Hazel. If there's anything else I can do, just tell me. But for now I think I'm just going to lay low for a while. Get myself back on track. Try not to wreck anyone else's marriage.'

In spite of everything, Ben's comment made me smile.

'I think that's a very good idea indeed.'

Chapter 25

It was down to Gemma and Eliot now. I'd lain awake the last two nights worrying about it – the guilt that my brother seemed to have played some part in Eliot losing his job, and the panic that I'd been counting on the wedding business working, and it all now seemed to be falling apart. I'd put the set I'd made for the Highlands wedding to the back of my cupboard, trying to accept that it might now never become reality.

That evening I busied myself with tidying the spice cupboard at home, and cleaning the oven. I couldn't stop thinking about the two of them and how and why it had all gone so wrong. And whichever way I looked at it, I felt I was to blame. There were cheaper venues to go for – cheaper suppliers, simpler dresses that Gemma still would have looked stunning in ... I'd got carried away with my own vision of their dream wedding just as much as Gemma had. I'd been so busy dressing the beautiful set, I'd neglected to pay any attention to the actor and actress who were the only reason for the play. A thought nagged at me. Even if we got some of the money back, the deposits were gone. I'd been so eager to pin everything down, make sure we didn't miss our chance – I hadn't once considered what might happen if it all fell through.

'Cleaning the oven again? Have things got that bad?' Amber asked.

'Yes. I think they have.'

'Wedding planning?'

'Sort of. Not sure if I'll even have one to plan for at this rate.'

'Oh dear,' Amber said. 'Stop that for a minute and come and sit down. Give me an update.'

I brushed my hair out of my eyes, then filled Amber in on what had been happening.

'I'm worried about them, but I'm also worried about me,' I admitted. 'I was counting on this wedding working out, not least so that I could start to build up a portfolio to show potential clients. My Dad's invested in me, and I'm about to be unemployed. I can't afford for this to fall through, Amber.'

She gave me a hug. 'It'll work out. I'm sure of it.'

'I really hope so – because I don't have a Plan B.'

*

'All set?' Josh asked, at work the next day.

I nodded, and Josh and I walked out of the office building. I was in the final week of my notice period, and nerve-wracking as it was, I was ready to leave Twenty-One for good. There were certain things I'd miss. But now that I was leaving, I realised I wouldn't miss the work that much. It had fascinated me at the start, but as time had gone on I'd started to disengage, and it felt a little like I imagine it must feel leaving someone you've fallen out of love with. There was only one person I was really sorry to be losing daily contact with – and that was Josh. Whether we were at the office or out on location, a smile from him had brightened my day on so many occasions. I knew what it was like, when you left. I didn't want us to be those colleagues who had drifted in and would drift out of each other's lives. Which was why I was so happy he'd suggested we duck out for a while.

'Seeing as it's such a nice day, shall we get take-out coffees, and go across to the park?' he suggested.

'Sounds good.'

We found a bench by the bandstand partly shaded by a large oak tree. A group of men and women were practising Tai Chi a few metres from us, casting geometric shadows on the lawn, a scattering of brown and gold leaves surrounding them.

'I feel like I'm bunking school,' I said, taking a sip of my coffee – strong with plenty of frothy milk and a trace of cinnamon, just how I liked it.

Josh laughed. 'I know what you mean. We should do this more often.'

Josh leaned back on the bench, closing his eyes for a minute and soaking up the sun rays on his face. I noticed the flash of collarbone showing through above his shirt.

I looked away, focusing my attention on the Tai Chi brigade.

'I'll miss you, when you go,' Josh said.

'Awww, thank you,' I said. A flush of warmth came to my chest. 'I won't be leaving town. I'll still be here. We can still hang out.'

'You'll be free,' Josh said, playfully. 'You won't want to be reminded of this place.'

I will, I thought. Some parts of it.

'We can meet for lunch. I'll tell you about the triumphs and disasters of going it alone in the wedding planning business.'

'I know you're going to make a great success of it. I hope you'll continue to design sets, alongside it . . . you're too talented to give that up.'

I thought of the miniature sets tucked away in my closet. I would never stop working on them. They were the twin tracks my life ran on, parallel worlds where everything went smoothly.

'Anyway, Hazel,' Josh said, a directness in his voice as he sat up straight again. 'There was something I wanted to talk to you about.'

'Yes?'

'Yes. You know the last few weeks, when we've been talking . . .'

I nodded.

'The truth is, when I was asking you about everything you're doing, outside of work, I mean – it's because I'm genuinely interested.'

He paused, and glanced down. 'The thing is, I know already, from the work that we've done together, that you're talented – you have a great artistic eye, and I don't know . . . you just seem to pull the strings on the generally dysfunctional marionette that is the art department and make it all perform very well.'

I laughed. 'No one's ever described me like that before.'

'You're great at what you do. Everyone thinks so.'

'Thanks. Well, except Emma, perhaps,' I said, with a smile.

He rolled his eyes. 'The only person Emma thinks is great is Emma. Although of course, I never said that.'

'And of course I never nodded in agreement,' I said, nodding.

'Hazel,' he said. 'Something a bit crazy happened last night. Or rather it's about to happen.' He stumbled over the words, rubbing the space between his eyebrows.

I waited for him to continue and started to wonder where this conversation was going.

'Sarah was outside my bedroom window last night. Stereo blaring out a song we used to listen to when we first met, carrying a rose,' he smiled. 'And she proposed to me.'

My breath caught. 'And you said . . .'

'I said yes,' he said.

'Congratulations,' I managed. It was harder to get the word out than I'd expected. I shouldn't care like this. I really, really shouldn't care that Josh was getting married. I kept my smile in place and hoped it looked more convincing than it felt.

'Sarah was right. We do need to change something. And maybe this is it. I guess there's no point waiting. She wants to get married by the end of this year, and it's September already. This morning I woke up panicking about how we're going to fit everything in.'

So *this* was where it was going.

'We could really use some help. Sarah loved the sound of your sister's wedding, and obviously I already know you're a creative genius,' he said, with a smile. 'Please say you'll agree to be our wedding planner?'

The words hung there in the air for a moment, while I gathered my thoughts. What I'd felt, what I thought I'd felt, worried I'd felt, in the days before Lila's wedding – it hadn't been anything real. Just a stupid, fleeting – crush, I suppose –

if that. Josh and I had a connection, yes, we always had. But as friends, nothing more.

I didn't want to do this. No part of me wanted to agree. But I fought back the feeling. I'd get used to it. I had to think of the business. Especially now the one wedding I'd been commissioned to plan, Gemma and Eliot's, was hanging in the balance.

Josh had a look of wide-eyed anticipation on his face, and I realised I'd left him hanging.

'Of course,' I said. The words didn't come easily, or steadily though. 'Thanks for thinking of me. It would be a pleasure.'

Chapter 26

At the end of the week, I packed my personal belongings into a box, and prepared myself to walk out of the Twenty-One offices for the final time. When I glanced behind me, I saw Amber watching me, concern in her eyes.

'You OK?' Amber mouthed.

'Oh, fine,' I mouthed back, nodding. She looked unconvinced.

All I have to do is do this without getting upset, I told myself.

Then I saw Josh coming over to my desk, with a giant card and a hamper. 'We couldn't let you go without saying a proper goodbye,' he said, handing them over.

I opened the card and saw dozens of notes wishing me well, and each familiar name made me smile. When I looked up, a crowd of my colleagues had formed around my desk. A lump came to my throat.

'You're very kind,' I said, looking down at the overflowing food and drink hamper. 'I'm going to miss working here.'

'We're very sorry to see you go,' Aaron said. 'You are one of the best. The door will always be open.'

'Thank you,' I said. A flicker of doubt crept into my mind. I was leaving all this – people I liked and job security, and heading into . . . Well, I didn't know what.

Amber seemed to pick up on it and whispered in my ear. 'Don't worry,' she reassured me. 'You're going on to bigger and better things.'

People said their goodbyes and headed back to their desks. I went to get my coat, and Emma called me over. She hadn't been there earlier, and after what had happened, I'd wondered if she'd even say goodbye.

I readied myself for a brusque farewell, but instead, her voice was soft.

'I'm sorry you're leaving, Hazel,' she said, simply. 'And I'm sorrier that it's my fault.'

Now this – this I hadn't been expecting.

'I know I've been a nightmare to work for these past few months. There are no excuses. All I can say is this – you leaving, you, one of the most talented people at this company – and knowing that I'm at least partly responsible for that, has been a real wake-up call for me. I need to pull myself together and make a new start.'

'Right,' I said, feeling startled. 'Well, I appreciate that.'

'And while I can't undo what I've done, I want to make sure you have the best possible new start too. So you'll get a glowing reference from me, don't worry about that. And while I'm not the greatest believer in marriage,' she said, a jaded look returning to her eyes, 'it seems a great many of my friends are hurtling headlong into it. I might even be able to pass a few clients your way.'

She smiled, and I thought, for a moment, that I saw a glimmer of humanity there.

On the journey home, I thought about how the morning had gone. I appreciated the kind goodbyes, but now that I was out of the office I felt surer than ever that I was heading in the right direction. I had just got home when my phone rang: Eliot.

He said he needed to talk, and sounded desperate. I arranged to meet him by the canal and headed down there right away.

I caught sight of him, down by the boats, in jeans and a sweater, his face unshaven.

'Don't tell me,' he said. 'I already know it. I'm an idiot.'

'Well, yes,' I said. 'You are a bit. What happened to you? Where did you go? Gemma's absolutely devastated. What's more she hasn't got any idea at all what's going through your mind.'

Eliot shook his head, as if he was trying to shake away all

of the bad feeling caused by unpicking the joyful things in his life, and the future he had planned.

'Is this to do with losing your job?'

'Sort of. Yes. No. I just know it's a mess,' Eliot said. 'This isn't how I wanted things to be when we got married.'

I led him over to a bench, and we sat down. I stayed quiet, waiting for him to speak again. I had to stay objective – even if seeing Gemma looking so broken made that a challenge.

'Now – just to be clear,' I said. 'If you allow Gemma to help you, you'd still be able to afford the wedding you both planned, right?'

'Yes,' he said, bashfully. 'Gemma has savings that could cover everything she wants to happen.'

'But you won't let her.'

He shook his head. 'No. It would be official then – everyone would know I'd failed her, let her down.'

'Don't be ridiculous,' I said. 'And no one needs to know. It's nobody's business but yours. Stop being so self-centred.'

It seemed to jolt him out of his self-pity. 'What?'

'You're going to throw away the love of a wonderful, beautiful and talented woman, rather than let her know you're short on funds? I bet Gemma wouldn't care less if you got married in the local registry office and went to Pizza Express afterwards.'

Eliot raised an eyebrow.

'OK – maybe I got carried away,' I said, biting my lip.

Gemma in a Top Shop white dress tucking into a Sloppy Giuseppe on the day of her nuptials was a little hard to picture. 'Yes, she's going to want the big wedding you've planned, but you've already suggested there might be other ways to finance that. If you're willing to put your pride to one side.'

He shrugged. 'It's not just the money ... it's ... she'll see me differently, us differently.'

'Don't you think she already does – sitting there in her flat with your things half-packed up, thinking that you're having an affair or God knows what else?'

'Oh no ... she doesn't think that, does she?' Eliot said, looking even more heartbroken.

'Go and talk to her, Eliot. You need to fix this, and fast.'

That Friday night, I met with Sarah and Josh at the pub for our first discussion about their wedding.

Josh pulled out a chair for Sarah, and we all sat down. I was going to be strictly professional – Josh might be a friend, but he and Sarah were now clients who I had to strive to impress, just like any other.

'We don't want a Christmassy thing – not at all,' Sarah said.

'I mean, I had thought about having it in our local church back home, the one where Mum and Dad got married ...' Josh's eyes brightened as he spoke about it.

'It's not right for us,' Sarah said, briskly. 'Far too conventional.'

'So, yes,' Josh said. 'We thought it would be better to get married abroad.'

I could see the disappointment in Josh's eyes as he resigned himself to the compromise. I wondered if I should step in, urge them to discuss it again before dismissing the idea of a wedding in the UK. Sarah's voice interrupted my thoughts.

'Christmas is a good time for people to travel,' Sarah said brightly. 'Take some proper holiday. And that's the plan – a big beach party. It's just so me and Josh, you see. We're not the church bells type. Not at all.'

'Actually my family are – sort of. But I'm sure they'll come round to the idea when we tell them the plans.'

'OK, great,' I said. 'We can really have some fun with this one, I think. Did you have any particular locations in mind?'

'Somewhere hot,' Josh said. 'That's as far as we've got really, isn't it, Sarah?'

'I'd love to go to India . . . somewhere like that.'

Josh raised an eyebrow.

'I *know*,' she said to him. 'Don't worry, I'm over it now. Josh's family would never come round to that idea.'

'What are your main criteria,' I said. 'You mentioned a beach?'

'Yes,' Josh said. 'A beach, somewhere with good food, that's going to be hot. We'd need some nice accommodation nearby too. My grandmother's going to be there and unfortunately she's not able to walk that far, so we'd need you to bear that in mind when it came to the venue.'

Sarah got out a scrapbook and put it on my desk. 'Here were some ideas I had.'

I opened it to see a magazine collage of beach scenes and people juggling fire. Orange lilies and pools of koi carp with little wooden bridges over them.

'Would you want the ceremony itself to be outside? I'd just need to look into how we make sure it's all legal. Or you could always do the legal bit somewhere else.'

'We'd be happy to do the legal bit first,' Josh said. 'We don't really mind where, we just want somewhere special to say our vows.'

'OK,' I made a note. 'That's great. That makes things easier – so I'll still be able to find somewhere nice for you, but we really have free rein then on a fantastic location for you to have the ceremony with all your friends and family.'

Josh passed me a sheet of paper. 'This is the budget we're looking at. We're hoping that should cover it.'

I had to stop my jaw dropping. 'Yes, that looks fine. Even with the tight deadline – I should be able to present you with some really good options working to this figure. Now – you say you've ruled out India. Is there anywhere else that you'd like me to look into when I draw up some ideas for you?'

'We were thinking of the Caribbean.'

'Antigua,' Sarah said.

'Cuba.'

Josh and Sarah's answers came in unison, and they started to laugh.

'Both of those are options,' Josh explained.

'Excellent,' I said. 'Any theme you had in mind?'

'No,' Sarah said, shaking her head vigorously. 'Can't think of anything worse. We just want something chilled out, low key, informal. We want our guests to be comfortable wearing what they want, just hanging out.'

Josh glanced at Sarah and then back at Hazel. 'But we might need to retain a few traditional touches,' he said, gently. 'You know, for my mum and dad. They are a bit more old school than Sarah's family. They'll be expecting the usual run of things – ushers, top table, that kind of thing.'

'OK,' I said. 'Like I said, we don't have much time on this, so we might just need to get started on choosing a venue and we can decide on some of the other aspects of the day as we go along. Does that sound all right to you?'

Josh and Sarah nodded.

'I'll start researching venues for you now. I'll send the details over and then let's talk again.'

Chapter 27

'So – tell me,' Amber said. 'What's she like? Josh's Sarah?' Her eyes were wide and curious.

'Why are you so interested?' I asked.

'Everyone's interested, aren't they? The way Josh talks about her, it's like she's practically another member of the office.'

'She's nice,' I said with a shrug. 'And pretty, I guess. If you like that tousle-haired, tanned, fiery, glittery-eyed kind of . . . well yes, I suppose by anyone's standards she's pretty. And she's bright, funny . . .' I tried to keep things positive. Yes, there were things about her I was less keen on, but to dwell on those would be . . . well, unhelpful and unkind. Josh was marrying Sarah.

'He seems happy?'

'Yes, I think so.'

'I would have thought this would be a challenging one,

eh. With her being such a traveller and Josh's parents . . .'

'What about Josh's parents?' I asked.

'Apparently they're super-traditional,' Amber said, matter-of-factly. 'You know he's from money, right?'

'Is he?' I asked. It had never come up, and while he was well-spoken, and seemed like perhaps he'd seen the inside of a theatre once or twice, it still surprised me. He was always so humble. Plus his bike was crap.

'Oh yes. Dad's a lord or something. Didn't he ever tell you that?'

I shook my head. I felt a pang of envy that he'd confided in Amber, but never in me. We'd talked often enough, hadn't we, for him to make mention of it?

'Not that he told me, of course. One of the work experience girls had a crush on him and it came up when she Googled his name. Adding the workies on the tea round has its pay-offs, you see.' Amber smiled. 'Massive pile in the country, apparently. I'm kind of surprised they wouldn't be having the wedding there.'

It seemed increasingly odd that Josh hadn't said a word.

'I guess they want to leave that all behind,' I said. 'I can understand that. Probably a lot of expectations that come with it. Getting away from it all, well there are benefits to that, aren't there?'

Josh was a low-key kind of guy, and clearly had made his own way in life rather than living off whatever funds his parents had. It made sense that he would want to have the wedding independently too. Infuriatingly, it all made me warm to him a little bit more.

I moved through images on my Macbook, researching tours for Josh and Sarah to go on after their wedding. We'd settled on Cuba.

One was a tour of a coffee plantation, with accommodation on a stunning hacienda surrounded by lush scenery. I could just picture the two of them relaxing in the hammocks.

Planning Josh and Sarah's wedding still felt very strange. Picturing them there on the beach, taking their vows to be with each other for ever. It was what all three of us were working towards, and yet my feelings were conflicted.

I'd arranged to meet Josh at the pub on the corner, to update him, so I packed my laptop and left the flat.

'Hazel, I really appreciate you stepping in like this. I know it must all seem a bit crazy ...'

We took our drinks back over to the table, and I steeled myself to ask the question. 'No more than any wedding is,' I smiled. 'Look, I don't want to be nosy ... but when we were talking the other day, I realised I don't know a thing about your family. Are they OK about the wedding happening abroad?'

Josh looked a little distant for a moment, and his brow

furrowed. 'Oh they will be,' he said. He seemed uncertain, though. He shrugged. 'They know what Sarah's like. Strong-minded. My mum and dad respect that in her.'

'Cool,' I said. 'And you're sure there's nowhere, like a family home . . . you might want to, you know, consider . . .'

Josh looked at me and rolled his eyes skyward. 'Right. My secret's out,' he said, laughing.

'Sorry.' I felt sheepish. I should have known I wouldn't be able to get away with such obvious snooping.

'I don't think my family home would be right for our wedding, even if it is what my family want. It's . . . I don't know. Showy, I guess. And Sarah would hate it, of course.'

'Fine. I shouldn't have pried.'

'It's fine,' Josh said warmly. 'But it's just not relevant.'

'OK,' I said.

'You're bothered that I didn't tell you, aren't you?' he asked.

I couldn't hold it in any longer. 'You're the son of a lord and you just didn't think to mention it?'

He shrugged. 'I bet there's a ton of stuff I don't know about your family.'

I suppose that was true.

'Sarah hates it all, anyway,' Josh said, glancing over to the bar.

I stayed quiet, waited for him to say more.

'Everything about my family,' he said. I couldn't read him,

210

but something in his expression told me it wasn't as comfortable a truth as he was making out. 'She says it's the money, the airs and graces, whatever, but they really aren't like that. I think she feels judged by them ... even though she has no reason to feel that way.'

'Maybe she'll come around,' I said.

'That's what she's saying about all this – that once we're married she knows she'll feel more settled, calmer about everything, including my family. It sounds weird, but ...'

'I understand,' I said. 'I got that sense from her. She certainly seems to love you a lot.'

I said the words, which were true, and felt a raw place open up inside my chest.

That night, at home, I got out a new empty box and my set-making equipment and started putting together the beach ceremony scene. I lined the aisle with tiny flowers, and made an arch out of twine. There was an uncomfortable feeling that wouldn't shift. I didn't want it to be Sarah there. I wanted it to be me.

Chapter 28

That Sunday I went down to Columbia Road flower market.

'Two bunches of roses for a fiver.'

The call rang out clearly in the crowded Hackney streets. I walked on the cobblestones of Columbia Road, taking in the sights and smells of the flower market, looking for inspiration. I was going to put together a couple of bouquets and extras to photograph for the website I was putting together. I'd already written most of the content and compiled a grid of links to other sites that I wanted to include. Amber had offered her help on the techy side of things.

Now I just had to – I scanned all the blooms, then smiled to myself. I just had to pick out the flowers I liked, and that I thought would look most beautiful. On a bright Sunday morning, it didn't seem much like work at all.

'Hey,' I turned at the familiar voice, and saw Gemma

hurrying to catch up with me. Over the past week I'd purposely put her and Eliot out of my mind – I didn't want to interfere with problems that had gone way past the colour of bridesmaids' hair accessories.

'Hazel,' she said breathlessly.

'Hi.' I kissed her on the cheek.

'Have you got time for a coffee?' she said.

'Yes, sure.' The flowers would wait, and I could gamble on there being some last-minute bargains.

We got outside seats at a nearby café, ordered drinks and looked out onto the lively throng of hipsters, locals, excitable tourists and seasoned gardeners. 'I love it here,' I said, to break the silence.

'Yes,' Gemma said. Her voice was calm, her tone a little more muted than usual. 'I needed a breath of fresh air this morning. This place always reminds me that there are such beautiful things in the world if you just take the time to look for them.'

I waited a moment for her to speak, then, when she didn't, filled the quiet once more.

'How are things with Eliot. Have you spoken?'

She nodded. 'That's why I wanted to talk to you. I've been wanting to phone, but, well, everything's been such a muddle I guess it's easier to explain face to face.'

I nodded, hoping desperately that the muddle she'd mentioned wasn't beyond fixing.

'Eliot came and spoke with you, then?'

'Yes. Thanks for telling him to. I just can't get over how much worse he made things by keeping quiet. You heard me the other day – I was convinced he'd found someone else. So he lost his job? Who cares?'

My face broke into a smile, instantly.

'He hated the bloody place anyway,' Gemma said, shaking her head. 'I mean, yes – we were counting on the money to finance the wedding, but the last thing I want is for him to feel trapped somewhere because of that. I didn't work this hard for the past decade for nothing – I wanted to have the money and independence for the things that really mattered to me. I wouldn't care if Eliot was a skint artist, or a bin man, or a barista. He's Eliot. And I'm totally in love with him.'

The passion she spoke with filled me with hope and happiness, and I suppose if I'm honest, just a little bit of envy.

'I still want to marry him,' Gemma said, welling up. 'Of course I still want to marry him. And now I know that he wants to marry me just as much.'

A wave of happiness and relief swept over me.

'Great,' I said. 'You sound happy.'

'I'm over the bloody moon, Hazel. I've missed him so much.'

'And he's missed you, too.'

'Oh, and here's a surprise. Eliot's not going to look for another job.'

'What?' My chest tightened.

She must have sensed my discomfort as she quickly chimed in. 'Don't worry. It's fine. I mean – it's crazy, but it will be fine. He's going to train as a pilot. He's always wanted to do it, and I've managed to convince him that now's the time.'

'Wow,' I said, surprised. 'That's amazing.'

'Yes. He got his licence years ago, but it's stayed as a hobby. Now he wants to see if he can make a living out of it.'

'And you're behind him on this?'

'One hundred per cent. He's my Eliot, no matter what, and to see him like this – full of enthusiasm again. It's amazing, Hazel. He's like the man I first met.'

That evening, I picked up Gemma and Eliot's wedding folder again, and started to plan.

When I came out of my bedroom at dinnertime, I saw Amber in the kitchen, apron on and her hair in a loose bun on the top of her head. Beside her on the counter were trays of cupcakes, ready to go in the oven.

'You've been busy,' I said. I drank in the sweet cinnamon and ginger scent of them as I walked up to her. 'Who are all of these for?'

'You, if you want,' she said, looking up with a smile. It

didn't go quite as far as her eyes, though, which were missing their usual bright glimmer.

'You made all of these, for nobody in particular?' I asked, confused. Even for a baking aficionado like Amber, this was not usual.

'Mm-hmmm,' she said, with a shrug. 'Let's call it culinary therapy.'

Amber opened the oven to put them in, letting out a blast of heat that pushed me back a step.

She took off her oven gloves and sat down at the table, pulling out the chair beside her.

'He's in love with you,' she said, matter-of-factly.

'Who?' I said, flummoxed. This wasn't a sentence that got said. No one was ever in love with me. I wasn't one of those women. I don't know when that got set in stone, but I knew that it just *was*.

'Sam,' Amber said. His name – familiar but made curious and surreal by the context, hung in the air between us.

'He told me this evening. I've been an idiot, Hazel. I should have known it – and I should never have risked our friendship over it. But it's great – I mean for you – you, the two of you could be something awesome. You've always got along so well.'

'What . . .?' I said, feeling dizzy and muddled. 'I absolutely do not understand what's going on here.'

'Sam. He said he got it all back to front. He thought it was me he liked – but all along it was you. That perhaps it had always been you. He freaked out about losing your friendship but then once he was with me he seemed to lose it anyway, and that was when he saw how much he missed you.'

'Right,' I said, slowly taking it all in.

'So – in short – it's you he wants.'

'I'm sorry,' I said to Amber. 'You know I had no idea.'

'Of course I do,' she said. I saw she was upset, and felt bad about it – I'd led her into this situation after all. Sam was my friend.

'OK, cupcakes are great, but really I think it's too much pressure to put on even your baking to expect them to fix this. I'm going to pour us some gin and tonics,' I said, getting to my feet and grabbing some ice cubes from the freezer. I sliced into a lemon and lime, and filled two tumblers with the drinks.

'Thanks,' she said, taking it gratefully. 'Two days, that's all it'll take,' Amber said. 'I'm definitely not spending longer than that caught up in this.' She took a sip of the drink and winced slightly at the strength of the alcohol. 'Actually,' she said with a smile. 'Make that two hours.'

I sipped from my own glass. I felt bad thinking it – it's not like I would have wished for things not to work out – but the truth was, it was actually kind of nice having Amber back. I'd missed our weekend brunches, and night-time cups of cocoa while working our way through the *Breaking Bad* box set.

'We talked for a while,' Amber said. 'We were out – just like any other night, and the atmosphere just turned kind of serious. I thought he was going to ask if we could ramp things up a notch, I've been waiting for that kind of a discussion. Instead he started reminiscing about school, how you guys used to be so close, and saying that he really missed that. It took a few minutes for the penny to drop.'

It was awkward – I cared about Amber, yet suddenly she was the only gateway to understanding Sam's feelings. And I needed to know what they were.

'He was nice about it. As nice as he could be, given what he was actually saying. I guess it just took being with me to make him realise what he really wanted. Which means I should definitely get a mention in your wedding speech.' Amber forced a smile.

'You know that's not going to happen,' I said, shaking my head. 'Not to Sam, not to anyone.'

Amber looked at me, her smile melting away. 'Seriously though, Hazel. I know I've kind of muddled things, but you shouldn't let that distract you. I would never want to stand in your way. You stepped back, and now it's my turn. You should give him a chance.'

My heart was racing, but my head was foggy. I thought of Sam's face – his close-cropped light hair, dark eyebrows, blue-grey eyes, the skate clothes he still wore, even though he was a decade older than most of the kids in the park these days. It blurred into Josh's, and then back. I loved Sam. I'd always loved Sam. I'd never shared my life with any man like I had with him. And Josh – no, it wasn't worth going there. I had to draw a line under anything I'd once considered. Josh was getting married. And Josh – he'd probably be as excited as I was starting to feel about the prospect of Sam and me finally getting together.

'I feel terrible that he's messed you around,' I said to Amber.

'Oh he was perfectly nice about it,' Amber said. Her expression had started to soften, though. 'In so far as he could be, anyway.'

'Right,' I said.

'He's not the most mature person I've ever met, but then again neither are you.'

I wrinkled my nose at her, making a face.

'And that's the reason I like you both.'

'OK, you pulled it back there.'

Amber continued. 'You know what. I didn't know what I wanted when we got together. I still miss Jude badly. I just went with my gut feeling. Because who the hell does know what's right for them until they give it a go?'

Her words gave me pause for thought. I'd been ready to take that step with Sam just a few weeks ago, and it was only because of Amber that I'd shut my feelings off. Maybe I could be open to it again.

'I told him he should call you,' Amber said.

'Right.' I drew in my breath. It felt as if everything was about to change, and now part of me desperately wanted things to stay the same. I thought of my phone over on the coffee table and felt a powerful urge to switch it off – to avoid the whole situation.

'Put yourself first for once, Hazel,' Amber said. 'You deserve something good. Maybe this is it.'

I went to bed that night, soft tartan pyjamas and bedsocks making things seem a little more familiar and comfortable even now they were starting to change, and I put my mobile on the bedside table. I loved and hated that mobile in equal measure right now.

I checked it one more time – no calls, no messages. Then eventually slipped into sleep.

Chapter 29

On Tuesday evening, I went to meet Lila just outside the studio she rehearsed in. Even though I knew it was only a matter of minutes before she and her fellow dancers would flood out, flushed and excited after their afternoon rehearsing, I checked my phone. No messages, none from Lila, none from Sam. Lila had had an audition earlier in the week, and today was the day she was due to find out whether she'd got the part of Clara in *The Nutcracker*.

The door swung open and I saw the familiar faces of a couple of her friends, they came down the stairs chattering animatedly to one another. Then Lila – I saw her and she raised her hand in greeting. I desperately tried to read her expression.

She walked over to me.

'So?' I asked eagerly.

She shrugged, then looked down. She shook her head sadly.

I felt as if it were happening to me just as much as her. A stab of disappointment in my gut – and disbelief.

'No . . .' I said.

She glanced up and there was a twinkle in her green eyes. 'I had you there, didn't I?' she said, smiling.

'You got the part?'

'Yes,' she said, beaming. 'You're looking at Clara.'

I swept her into my arms and hugged her close. We jumped up and down on the spot, both letting out squeals of excitement. We could have been eight years old right then – and everything in the world – everything – was just right.

When I got back to the flat, my phone buzzed with a call. I took a breath, checked the name on the screen, and answered it.

'Sam, hi,' I said.

'Hazel.'

'How's it going?' I asked, as if I knew nothing, though he must surely have realised that Amber's words would filter back to me.

'I've got tickets for a film this weekend. I was wondering if you'd like to come with me.'

My heart beat fast in my chest.

'Rooftop cinema. I thought it might be up your street.'

I smiled. 'Sounds good.'

'Great,' he said, with audible relief.

'What time?'

'Starts at eight. I'll pick you up at yours.'

'OK,' I said.

The conversation was drawing to a close and I still didn't know where we were.

'Sam . . .' I started.

'Yes,' he said. I could almost hear him blush. 'It's a date. I hope you're OK with that?'

'Right,' I said, my heart racing. 'Yes, I'm OK with that.'

Amber and I were sitting watching *Modern Family* with a vat of popcorn, when I decided to fill her in.

'So, I spoke to Sam,' I told Amber. Whatever happened, we were living together and I didn't want to keep any secrets from her.

'Yes?' She looked genuinely interested and excited for me.

'We're going on a date. This weekend.'

'That's good,' she said.

'I'm not sure how it will all pan out,' I said, honestly. 'But going feels right. I'm just sorry you got stuck in the middle with this. I was a bit blind to what was really going on, I guess.'

'We all have moments of that,' Amber said. 'And don't worry about me. I'm like a bouncing ball with this stuff. I've just signed up with a dating site, as it happens.'

'You have? That was quick.'

'Haven't finished my profile yet. God, it's tricky, isn't it. Making yourself sound interesting but without looking like a total weirdo?'

'Do you want me to give it a look over? I bet you're underselling yourself.'

'Would you? Thanks. I'm just choosing a photo and then I'll show you.'

'Cool. No news from Jude?'

'No. Nothing,' she said. 'Much easier that way.'

'It must be.'

'Well, not absolutely nothing. My friend Heather bumped into him, and they talked a bit. She said he asked what I was up to . . . but that's it. I didn't ask her anything about him. I don't want to know.'

Amber seemed keen to change the subject.

'I've hurt enough over him,' she said.

That week I thought about Sam almost constantly. He was there in my mind when I woke, and as I lay my head back on my pillow at night, I imagined his head next to mine. Those familiar blue-grey eyes. The warm skin of his arms, shoulders that I'd touched before, but on different terms. I wished away the weekdays, and longed for Friday to come.

When Friday finally arrived, Sam picked me up at mine.

We went to a rooftop cinema screening. We sat on

deckchairs and drank margaritas and laughed through the film. It was *Pulp Fiction* and we'd both seen it a dozen times before. Between us we could have recited half the scenes, and I was kind of glad, because it meant that we could talk. When Sam passed me another drink, his hand grazed mine. He didn't move away, and neither did I.

We didn't talk about what he'd said on the phone, or about what had happened with Amber. As we sat there on a Hackney roof terrace surrounded by striped deckchairs and with the rattling of guns coming through loud on the speakers around us, it didn't feel right to talk over whether things were about to change, or if, perhaps, they had changed already. But I wanted to be close to Sam. I didn't want anyone coming between us, not now, not a stranger, certainly not another of my friends, not even the drunken teenager who was weaving her way to the toilets and pushing between our seats.

'Let's go for a drink after this,' Sam said to me as the credits rolled, his voice lower and quieter this time.

It wasn't a question, so I didn't answer, just nodded. We left the rooftop screening together, and my heart was racing in anticipation of what might come next.

A quarter of an hour later, Sam and I were sitting next to each other on the vintage leather sofa at the pub near my flat. It dipped a little in the middle, which I'd never really noticed before, but now, with my bare arm almost touching the skin of his, and our denim-clad thighs close, I felt incredibly aware of it. It wouldn't normally have mattered, we've shared personal space often enough before, but things felt different now. It had been on the cusp of happening for years, one way or another, but now it had finally happened. We weren't just friends any more, and both of us knew it. If Amber hadn't already told me, I think I would have worked it out myself by now.

'So I guess you're wondering why I wanted to meet,' Sam said.

I think I already know. I can't quite believe it, but I think I already know.

'I suppose.'

'I wanted to talk to you. I'm sorry everything turned into such a mess,' he said.

'It's a shame it didn't work out with Amber,' I said hurriedly. 'She's great.'

'She is,' he said, his eyes not even flickering away from me for a moment. It was starting to unnerve me a little. 'But I should never have asked her out. I only did it because I thought you wanted me to.'

'Why on earth would I want you to?' I said.

'You seemed to be hinting all the time about how nice she was. And after Christmas, well, you went so quiet. I thought you regretted what happened.'

'I never wanted you to go out with her. Of course I didn't. And yes – I did regret what happened at Christmas, because you totally went cold on me. Or have you forgotten all that?'

'I'm sorry I pushed you away,' he said.

Don't say it. I don't know what I'll do if you say it.

'Because I wanted you then. I just wasn't ready. I panicked. It was never about anyone else. It was always about you, Hazel.'

Then he covered my hand with his, and there was a bond between us again. There was a warmth in knowing it was me and Sam, after all the years that had passed, all the times we'd shared, drinking late into the night and talking, going out to the cinema together, skateboarding in the park. I knew him like no one else; he was almost part of me. And I knew, from the way he was looking at me now, that familiar connection sparked up with a new intimacy, and a longing, that he felt it too.

'I've been a bit lost lately. You know, back at home ... But now I know. I know you can sort me out. You're what I need. I want to be with you, Hazel. I want us—' his voice caught, and he coughed, the only sign of this being difficult for him. 'I want us to be together.'

He reached out to touch my face. I motioned with my hand for him to stop.

'I know you've thought about it,' he said. His voice was low and husky and it almost disarmed me totally.

'Of course I have,' I whispered. 'You know that.'

'Well how will we know, if we never even try?'

It felt good being with him. Talking with him. Laughing. His touch was always warm, tender, and I couldn't help but imagine how it would feel – taking it further, being together in the only way that we'd never tried.

And then – before I'd really thought about what was right or what was wrong – before I'd done anything more than just feel the attraction – we were kissing.

Chapter 30

The next morning, Amber and I had breakfast together. I still had the kiss with Sam on my mind. I'd felt swept up in it – swept up in him – but at the same time there was something about my lips on his that made me feel I'd been there before. When we'd moved away from each other he was still the same Sam, and I was still the same me, and yet everything had changed. We'd stayed up that night talking – and found our way back to being close again.

Amber told me she had her dating profile ready for me to look at.

'So, what do you think?' She passed me her iPad, with her profile open. She'd chosen a photo of her at a festival – straw hat on and her hair loose, the skin of her shoulders lightly tanned.

'Nice photo.' I said. 'You look . . .'

'More relaxed?' she said, voicing my thoughts.

'I guess, yes. Happy.'

'I was. Isle of Wight festival. I was there with Jude, but that doesn't matter, I cropped him out.'

'Cinema-loving fan of gin and tonics and late-night baking . . .' I read. 'Sums you up pretty well.'

'Could be either of us, now I think about it,' Amber laughed. 'What do you think about the longer blurb?'

I scanned over it. 'It's good,' I said, hesitantly.

'What?' Amber said. 'Come on, be honest with me, Haze. That's why I asked you.'

'You just seem to be holding your cards quite close to your chest, that's all,' I said. 'If you're going to go for this, maybe you need to really go for it.'

She breathed out slowly. 'Hmm. Maybe you're right. Urgh it all feels like such a minefield. I sometimes wish . . .'

'You can only go forward,' I said.

'I know. Give me that, I'm going to rewrite it.'

When Amber left, I rode my bike over to the park. There were no bluebirds accompanying me on my ride through the green space, there was no dizzy high or irrepressible smile. None of the things I'd been led to expect of love. Instead, well, it just felt OK, safe. Perhaps there was only so much one single kiss could bring.

Sam called me on the Tuesday, my second week of self-employment after working out my notice. We met up in a bar on the South Bank, close to the train station he'd come from, and alive that night with the buzz of friendship and new romance. We ordered wine and tapas at a bar overlooking the river, and it felt then as if we might be part of that buzz. Could we acknowledge it or would saying it out loud make the whole thing disappear?

'So how's it going with the P.E teaching?' I asked.

'Good,' he said, nodding. Silence fell between us for what must have been a minute but felt longer. 'You? How's your work?'

'Oh, it's coming together, yes.'

'What was it again . . . wedding planning?'

'Yes,' I said. 'I've got two weddings on at the moment – both for Christmas. It's busy, but the money's good and I really enjoy it.'

'Nice,' Sam said, vaguely. 'Still seems a bit strange to me. You. Weddings. You were never very girly like that, were you?'

I felt instinctively protective of my new career, and of the people whose wedding days I'd started to care about. 'It's an honour, really. To be asked to help with one of the most important days in these people's lives.'

'OK,' he said. 'I guess I see what you mean.'

We should shift away from work, I thought. It's totally unimaginative. Far more interesting to discuss the many other things that we have in common.

'So the cinema was fun the other night,' I said.

'Oh brilliant. Knew it would be. Sound wasn't that great up there though, was it? – and they must have shown an edited version, as it was missing a scene at the end.'

'Yes. Of course.' I didn't want to confess that I'd been kind of distracted that evening, not entirely focused on the film as I tried to figure out which direction our first date together might take.

'You noticed, right?' Sam said.

'Sure.'

'Not that it matters,' Sam said quickly. 'Not really. I mean I enjoyed the night. It was fun.'

I smiled.

'It feels good, doesn't it?' he continued. He reached across the table, taking my hand in his. 'You and me.' The touch of his hand sent a tingle through me.

I nodded. 'Yes. Yes it does.'

'I guess I couldn't see it before but—'

My phone, out on the table beside me, rang. I turned to see Sarah's name. I ignored it, and turned back to Sam, his blue-grey eyes on me.

I could do this. The talking about us. God, I'd waited long enough to do this.

'You can get that,' Sam said.

The phone rang off. Then the ringing started again, Sarah once more.

'It's a client,' I explained.

'Get it,' Sam said, sitting back in his chair. 'Honestly. It's fine.'

'Hey Sarah,' I said, picking up.

'I – have you got time to chat?' Sarah said, breathless on the phone. 'I've only got a little while, Josh is in the shower. But I had to talk to you.'

'Yes. Of course, Sarah. What is it? What can I help you with?'

'I know I shouldn't really be calling you, but I needed to talk to someone. Josh's family are being mental about this whole getting married abroad thing.'

'Right,' I said, getting to my feet and giving Sam an apologetic look. I walked a few steps away from the table towards the river, where it was quieter. 'What exactly is going on?'

'I mean, they've always been massively uptight. I couldn't say that when we met – but seriously. They really are. There's a side of him that's a bit like that too, but I like to think I'm slowly working it out of him. Anyway, this week things have really gone wrong. His grandmother always has to be the centre of things, and God help us, she's decided this whole wedding has to revolve around her. It's ridiculous.'

'Well, family are pretty important on a day like this,' I said, as diplomatically as I could.

'Not ours,' Sarah said. 'And it doesn't matter to Josh, either – I know him better than he knows himself sometimes.

He's just a natural people pleaser and finds it hard to say no. But there's absolutely no way I'm letting his family dictate how and when we get married. It's as simple as that.'

I heard a door open in the background.

'That's him,' Sarah whispered. 'I better go. I'll call you another time.'

I put the phone down and returned to the table. Our mains had arrived, and Sam was waiting for me.

'Sorry about that.'

He picked up his food and started to eat. 'It's OK,' he said.

I twirled the linguine I'd ordered around my fork, and tried to get back to being where we had been. But I got the feeling it wasn't as OK as Sam was making out.

Chapter 31

Later that evening, I came home to the flat on my own, and poured myself some peppermint tea. I'd said goodbye to Sam at the station and we'd arranged to see each other again that weekend. Somewhere quieter this time, where we could chat without any interruptions. It was still such early days and with other things going on it was hard to get a sense of if and how we might work in this new way.

I didn't feel ready for bed yet, and I was pleased when I heard the downstairs front door open. Ours opened a moment later, and Amber walked in.

I tried to read her expression.

'Disaster,' she said, slumping down on the sofa.

'That bad?'

'Worse,' she said, starting to laugh. 'He was totally self-obsessed. And seemed to think I was there just to smile and nod . . . I don't know. It just all felt a bit icky. And yet boring at the same time. God – have I been out of the game too long? Maybe I should be more patient, Haze. He didn't ask me a single question about myself. Not a single thing. I mean how rubbish is that?'

'Pretty rubbish,' I said. 'He sounds like a loser.'

'Ah well,' she said. 'Onward and upward.' She got out her mobile phone and swiped the screen. 'Courcheval78 just direct messaged me. What do you think?'

She showed me the guy on her screen, a smiling guy in his thirties with tanned skin, close-cropped mouse-brown hair and ski goggles on his head. 'Cute,' I said.

'He's asked if I'll meet him next weekend. I'm going to say yes.'

'Go for it.' It was inspiring to see how Amber never let life drag her down. She seemed to take each challenge or knock-back and build herself up better and stronger in response to it.

Right now she was smiling to herself as she tapped out a message. 'Done,' she said. 'God–' she looked at me. 'Listen to me, banging on about that dude being self-obsessed and I haven't even asked you about your evening. How did it go with Sam?'

'Oh good, thanks,' I replied.

'Good good? Amazing good? OK good?'

'I don't know. I feel like we didn't really have a chance to get started this evening. We were having some drinks by the river, I mean that was nice. But then I got this call from

Sarah, you know, Josh's Sarah – she needed advice on something . . . it kind of knocked the romance out of the evening.
There's nothing like someone's wedding stress to dampen
that, I guess.'

'Oh no – that sucks. Did you have to answer? I mean I
know your clients pay well, and Josh is a friend – but that
doesn't mean you have to be at their beck and call twenty-
four seven, surely. I mean, you did that with Emma, and I
thought that was what you were walking away from.'

'Maybe you're right. And when it comes to the stage
when we're talking through details of table decorations, I'll
make sure I keep my phone off in the evenings. But these are
big decisions, and I want to make sure that the person carrying any stress is me, not the couple who are getting married.'

'I see what you mean, and it's admirable,' Amber said. 'But
it seems a lot to take on.'

'I can do it,' I said. 'I want to do it. Which is why I'm
meeting with Josh tomorrow, to get this thing sorted out.'

Josh sat down, and ran a hand through his hair. 'God, it's
complicated this wedding stuff, isn't it?'

'What's up?' I said, feigning ignorance.

'Family. My grandmother, to be precise. To be honest,
none of my family are that keen on the idea of the wedding –
nothing to do with your plans – they were just expecting
something a lot more traditional. Anyway, the thing is that

Granny is really upset about it all. She says she's been looking forward to this day for years, and how can she be there when it involves getting on a flight . . . She's too old. I really should have talked to her about it earlier. She seemed OK – I mean, she went on holiday abroad a year ago but it seems like things have got worse for her. Obviously my family are with her on it; they think I'm being really selfish opting for a wedding abroad. Perhaps I am.'

'Oh dear, it sounds like you've been having an awful time of it,' I said. 'Your poor granny. But you're not being selfish.'

'Aren't I? I'm doing all this to make Sarah happy without really thinking about what was right for my family.'

'That isn't selfish,' I said.

'I guess I see what you mean,' he said. 'I hadn't really thought about it like that.'

'Have you talked to Sarah about it?'

'Yes. I think that's what's getting to me the most. I talked to her about it last night, told her we needed to find a compromise, work out a plan that everyone would be happy with.'

'What did she say?'

'She doesn't understand at all. She says it's our day and we need to do what's right for us. She says if I loved her I'd find a way to talk my family round. She's not willing to adjust things at all. She doesn't want to compromise.'

'Right.'

'Hazel. I'm really torn – I feel like I could hurt my family a lot over this.'

'It won't come to that, I promise,' I said. 'We'll find a way to make this work.'

Chapter 32

'Come up to mine?' Sam said. 'We can watch movies. It'll be like old times.'

It was somewhere quiet, like we'd agreed. It just wasn't exactly what I'd expected him to suggest.

'Your parents' house?'

'They're away. It'll be perfect,' he said, as if he was suggesting a night out at an exclusive club rather than free rein of a semi-detached house in the village where we grew up.

And now, a day on, here I was, back in Bidcombe, walking down his street, about to see him. I wasn't quite sure as what – his friend? His girlfriend? I'd stood in front of my wardrobe for half an hour working out what to wear, and had settled in the end for loose-cut jeans and a tight, dark green top with jewel buttons, my hair in a ponytail. I knew Sam too well to pretend to be anyone but myself, after all.

He answered the door with a smile and welcomed me inside. He held out his arms for a hug. My face pressed close into his chest and I caught that smell of vintage band t-shirt – as if it's absorbed the beer and smoke of a dozen nights out and then been washed clean with laundry powder, but never quite lost its history. He held me tightly, and kissed my head, letting his face rest there close to me for a while.

It all felt quite, erm, meaningful. And then we pulled away from each other.

'Beer?' Sam said.

I nodded. 'Yes please.'

We sat quietly together in his living room, drinking from bottles of Corona.

I was the one who broke the silence. 'So you're here for the time being, right?' I asked, looking around the living room. 'Nice that your parents don't mind.'

'Don't mind?' Sam said with a smile. 'My mum's over the moon.'

'She is?'

'Yep. I don't think she ever really got used to the empty house after me and my brother left. Dad's not thrilled about it, but she rules the roost.'

'So you're not planning on moving out?'

'Not any time soon,' he said. 'Why would I? Better food here, anyway.' He gave me a smile. 'Anyway, have you seen what rents are like? This works for me. It works for all of us.'

'Come on, Sam, you're nearly thirty, though.'

'OK, so I'm not where I thought I'd be,' Sam said. 'But I've got you now. You'll sort me out, Haze. I think you're already starting to.' He smiled his winsome, slightly lopsided smile.

I took a sip of my drink. I wasn't sure how I felt about what he was saying.

'Fancy watching a movie?' Sam asked.

'Sure.' The suggestion came as relief. 'Let's do that.'

That night we curled up on the sofa and watched *Sin City*. Then *Spiderman*. Then *The Dark Knight*. We'd seen them all before, but it didn't matter. This time we weren't sitting apart on the sofa, just our feet touching – we were together, my body pressed against his, and I could feel his chest rise and fall as I rested on it. I was with him. We were together, a couple. When my eyelids started to lower, I fell asleep right there.

The next morning, I was woken by the thud of letters hitting the doormat. I lay there on the sofa for a moment, careful not to move in case I woke Sam, who was snoring gently. It felt kind of nice, lying there with him. Waking up next to him in the morning. It wasn't something I'd done with anyone for a very long time.

After a moment or two of calm, he woke with a start, and I had to grab hold of the sofa to prevent myself getting dislodged.

'Sorry, Haze,' he said, running a hand through his hair. 'I was having a weird dream.'

I got up to seated, and straightened out my rumpled top. I suddenly felt uncomfortable, being here in Sam's parents' house. We hadn't even made it upstairs to his bedroom. Sam raised his body up from where he was lying and we both sat there for a moment, side by side on the sofa.

'Tea?' I suggested.

'Yes,' he said, quickly.

An hour later I was at the door, ready to leave.

'See you this weekend?' Sam said, as if everything was still on course, just how he would have wanted it to be.

'OK,' I said. I walked back to the train station. There were no bluebirds. And it didn't matter – or maybe it did. Just a little bit.

Chapter 33

Amber was getting ready to go to work as I came in the flat after spending the night at Sam's.

She was eating toast at the table, with a card open in front of her.

'So, bit of a mystery,' she said. 'Look at this.'

She passed me the card. There was a gift voucher inside. 'A day's training with Rosanna Delgare ...' I cast my mind back to a recent TV series on baking. 'Isn't she?'

'Yes,' Amber nodded. 'One of – if not *the* best pastry chef in Europe. She's over in the UK on a tour for her new book and running a couple of cake-designing workshops. Mum and I were talking about them – but as the stuff of dreams. The prices are astronomical.'

'So ... where did this come from?'

'I don't know – it's anonymous. Arrived yesterday at work,' she said. 'Came with the regular post.'

'No handwriting?'

Amber shook her head. 'It's all typed. I was thinking perhaps it was Tim – I mean I have been putting some long hours in recently … it would be kind of weird for him to send it in the post, but not out of the realms of the possible.'

'Perhaps it's a case of not looking a gift horse in the mouth. Just go and enjoy it.'

'Don't worry about that, I fully intend to,' she said, smiling. 'It's something to take my mind off the date with Courcheval78, anyway.'

'Not a winner?'

'Only skiing. Seriously – only skiing,' she said, slapping her hand on her forehead. 'I mean I should've known – last time I pick a man whose username is a resort.'

I smiled. 'Next time.'

'Yes. I'm kind of envious of you and Sam – not like that – but the fact that you already know each other. You can just get on with being cosy and together, and not deal with all of this cringy stranger stuff.'

'I guess,' I said.

'It's great you two have found each other – I'm sure you have what it takes to last.'

I knew I couldn't go on with things the way that they were. As much as I'd wanted it to happen, as much as I'd *willed* it to happen, being with Sam didn't feel right. When I'd dreamed about being with him, I'd felt complete, and he and I had both brought out the very best in each other. Two happy people making one happy whole. It had seemed impossible that things could be any other way – we worked so well as friends, after all, and if we were attracted to each other too, surely that was the whole package? But instead, we had turned out to be less than the sum of the parts. Our friendship seemed to have wilted, with our new relationship a poor substitute, and – what I couldn't ignore any longer – I felt less like the woman I wanted to be than ever. What we had wasn't what Lila, or Gemma, or Josh had. And I was sure now that it never would be.

I'd wanted so much to believe in it. So it was with a heavy heart that I'd called Sam and arranged to meet him in the village pub in Bidcombe.

'Cheers,' Sam said, raising his glass. I raised mine, and forced a smile.

Guilt lay heavily in my stomach as I thought of what I'd come here to do. How had everything changed so quickly? From a time that I would have done anything to be with Sam, when I felt full of sadness about him choosing Amber, to now, when I had what I thought I'd always wanted and was about to push him away.

'It's good to see you,' he said. He went to kiss me, and I moved my face gently away.

He raised his eyebrows in surprise. 'Right.'

'I'm sorry,' I said. He looked wounded.

'What's going on? Have I done something wrong?' he asked.

'No, you haven't done anything wrong.'

'Then what?'

'I think we should talk about this, about where it's going.'

'Sure, if you want. But it's pretty clear to me. I know what I want,' he said, his eyes bright. 'And it's you.'

'You really feel that, still?'

'I'm better with you. I'm not a mess when we're together.'

I shook my head. 'I can't fix you, Sam. And I'm not sure I really want to. I haven't even worked out how to fix myself.'

'So what are you saying? I thought you wanted this? Everything you said last Christmas ... Did you not mean that?'

'I did mean it. I wanted us to be together. Which is why I feel bad saying this now. But I don't think it's working. I think I preferred being friends, after all.'

Sitting there on the sofa, frowning, I thought how small he looked. How vulnerable. How very little like the Sam I'd once thought I was in love with.

He laughed, wryly. 'I wasn't expecting this. Not at all.'

'I'm sorry,' I said. 'I hope one day we can be friends again.'

'Maybe,' Sam said, vaguely. 'But after this? I feel like you messed with my head, Hazel. I don't want to be friends right now. Not any time soon.'

Chapter 34

I woke up to a morning that was cool and grey. I was tempted to close the curtains again and block out what little light there was. I settled for pulling the duvet up over my head and nestling down into the sheets until the alarm clock told me in its definite way that I had to get up and start work.

I knew I had done the right thing in ending it with Sam. But I didn't feel good. I felt bloody awful. The balloon of hope I'd once held had now popped and shrivelled up into a sad little mess of plastic. And it wasn't just that those film scenes with me and Sam – a shinier, romantic version of me and Sam – were never going to play out, it was the fact that I didn't even have him as a friend to talk about it with. And I knew I wouldn't for quite some time. I couldn't be close to him, talk to him, share things with him like I once had, after what had just happened. He was right – I had messed with his head. But it wasn't that clear-cut. The whole thing had confused me, too. I'd felt something – every time he looked at me, and each time his hand had grazed mine.

And as I remembered that feeling, the way my body had lit up at his touch. But it just hadn't been enough.

I got up and made myself a cup of tea, and tried not to let the guilt take over. I had never wanted to hurt Sam, but that's exactly what I'd ended up doing.

I wanted to shake off the feeling, get some perspective. So I did something I hadn't done in months. I put on my leggings and trainers, and headed out towards the park for a run. Building up speed gradually, I jogged over the bridge opposite our flat and across the canal with its scattering of riverboats and barges, and I was grateful for the cool rain that lashed my face and shoulders. In saying no to Sam, I wasn't just turning down the chance of being with him, I was saying that the very thing I'd been wishing for, for years, wasn't what I really wanted, after all.

My sight blurred as the rain grew heavier, and the leaves became a mass of greens, yellows and golds. By pushing Sam away I felt as if I was erasing a part of myself. First Lila, in her own natural and healthy way had broken away, then my job, and now my last scrap of comfort blanket had been thrown away too. And I wasn't entirely sure who I was going to be now.

*

I met Gemma and Eliot that afternoon, and felt clearer and more focused. It brought home to me how distracted I'd been by things with Sam. It might hurt now, but everything was better this way.

'So, the wedding's getting close now,' I said to them both, brightly.

'Yes – I can't believe it. It's gone so quickly,' Gemma said, biting the nail of her index finger. 'But we're all set up, aren't we?'

'Yes – the beautiful Highlands venue, the Ceilidh, an amazing cake, all the flowers . . . it's all under control,' I said. 'Everything's arranged. All you and Eliot need to do is turn up. And not change your minds. Promise me you won't change your minds?'

They looked at each other and smiled.

'No chance of that,' Gemma said. 'After everything we've been through to get here, there's no way we're turning back.'

Amber was in the bath when I got home, and I could hear her singing. She emerged wrapped in a fluffy white towel and smiled when she saw me.

'How was the course?' I asked.

'Brilliant,' she said, glowing. 'Imagine – having an expert like that on hand, I was able to ask her everything I wanted about cakes; got some excellent tips.'

'Sounds good.'

'And at the end of the day, we were almost like friends, really. So, there was one more thing I asked her.'

'What was that?'

'I asked her to check the records, tell me who booked the course for me. Said I needed to know.'

'Who was it?'

'It was Jude.'

Chapter 35

Lila handed me the tickets to *The Nutcracker* she'd got for me and Amber. 'Here you go.'

'Fantastic. Thank you. Can't wait to see it tomorrow night. How's it all been going?'

'Intense, exhausting, terrifying. But in short I'm not sure dream come true even covers it,' Lila said proudly, with a smile.

She looped her arm through mine, and we walked down the street together, the day was cool with a light mist. 'I need a break from thinking about it, though. Tell me about you.'

'Me? Well, hard at work with the weddings. Eliot and Gemma are getting really excited about theirs now. It's going to be fun.'

'Ollie and I can't wait. And how have things been, with Sam? Since you decided to call it a day?'

The memory hurt – a visceral acknowledgement that someone so key to my life up till now was going to be absent from it, at least for a while.

'It's better this way,' I said. And it was true. Things were simpler, without Sam, without the doubts, without the questions. Part of me still wished I could turn the clock back, undo the feelings I'd had, then he'd had, go back to the simple time when we wanted nothing more from each other than a chat and to hang out.

'You must miss him,' Lila said, quietly, her green eyes fixed on mine.

'I do,' I said, reluctant to say it but relieved when I had. 'But it was the right thing, moving on. I'd talked myself into a corner, thinking if he wasn't right for Amber, then he must be right for me – but there are more than two women in the world . . .'

'And there are more men out there too,' Lila said. 'Plenty of them. Believe me, now that I'm married I can't stop spotting them.' She laughed.

'Oh I don't know,' I said. 'I mean yes, of course there are, I'm not disputing that. But I wonder if maybe the world's divided up into those who are good at relationships, like you, and those of us who are better off on our own.'

Lila looked at me quizzically.

'You think you're destined to be on your own?' she said.

I shook my head, but I couldn't shake away the feeling –

that Lila had just voiced the doubt that had been nagging at me for months.

'Maybe,' I said finally. 'After all, if you are better at being by yourself, why not realise that early on, before you hurt anyone else.'

Lila looked at me sceptically.

'Haze. You've got it all wrong.'

Chapter 36

I looked down at the tickets in my hand. Row 5, seats S and T. December 11th. The name of the show – *The Nutcracker* – had a dusting of glitter on it. I'd been looking forward to tonight for weeks. Seeing Lila on stage at the Royal Opera House. It was huge for her, and I wanted to give her every ounce of my support.

Then I looked back at my phone, and Amber's message:

So sorry, Haze. Photo shoot running late. I can't make it tonight.

It was just after five, on the day of the performance, and I was sitting on the sofa with Pablo, stroking his soft fur.

That's OK, I texted Amber back. That's OK, I told myself. These things happened. Amber was at her mum's cake shop. Word about her designs was spreading, and drawing a lot of good publicity, and I knew today's shoot was important for the business. It wasn't just that aspect of her life that was flourishing, either. As Jude's anonymous, yet no-longer-anonymous gestures trickled in to Amber at work – flowers, deliveries of muffins and cakes, tickets to her favourite films, she seemed to be warming to him again. She was thinking about giving him a second chance.

I had pictured me and Amber walking through fairy-lit Covent Garden, and then sitting through the performance before getting drinks together, London coming alive in the build-up to Christmas. With Amber by my side, it wouldn't matter that everyone else was in couples. We'd be facing the Christmas-time romance together, delighting in our freedom from disappointing gifts and arguments about whose family to spend it with. At least that had been the plan.

I toyed with the idea of calling Mum and Dad, even though I knew they'd already seen it. But the timing would be tight, and I couldn't shift the feeling that it was a slightly desperate act. I didn't want them feeling sorry for me. I was an independent woman. I could go on my own, what was I even bothered about? I'd get to see Lila backstage afterwards, anyway.

The show started at 7 p.m. I had to pull myself together and get into the Christmas spirit before then. I owed it to Lila. I grated some of the best chocolate I had in the kitchen cupboard and made up a batch of warm hazelnut-flavoured hot chocolate to drink with some of Amber's cinnamon cookies.

This would do it. I poured the drink and tried to rally – I'd put on my best red dress. I'd go. I'd enjoy it.

I opened the door of number 11 on my Advent calendar and ate the bell-shaped chocolate. Then I opened the doors of 12, 13 and 14 and ate them all too.

I sat down on the sofa, the mug of hot chocolate in my hands, and started to think that maybe I'd be fine just as I was, in jeans and my oversized wool jumper. I wished Amber was around to nudge me out of the stupid self-pity. Because this wasn't getting me on a bus across town. And I wasn't feeling Christmassy at all. I tried one of the biscuits – crisp on the outside but fresh and soft on the inside. They were good. This, at least, was a start.

The intercom buzzed. Startled, I got to my feet and went over to it.

'Hi Hazel,' came a voice. 'It's me.'

It wasn't entirely clear, there was a little road noise in the background. It sounded like Ben.

'Hey,' I said back.

'I'll buzz you up.'

I heard the door click open and the sound of footsteps on the stairs. I opened the door to let him in. I wondered what he was doing back in London, and why he hadn't phoned.

Then I saw that it wasn't Ben approaching up the stairs at all – it was Josh.

'Hi,' he called out cheerfully.

It was good to see him – his jacket was turned up against the chill temperatures outside, but there was warmth in his smile. 'Arctic conditions out there this evening. Looks beautiful, though. Sorry to drop by unannounced, but there was something I wanted to give you. OK if I come up?'

'Of course,' I said, waving him in through the door. We paused for a moment, then he kissed me on the cheek. It was something we'd never done when we were working together, but now felt like a natural way to greet each other. His cheek felt cool. His chest brushed just the tiniest bit against mine, and a spark flickered through me. Just a silly physical reaction. That was all.

'I wanted to drop these in,' Josh said, passing me a folder.

I took them from him, trying to recall what they were likely to be.

'The photos,' he reminded me. 'You asked Sarah for some of the two of us, and our friends, you thought they might be nice for decorations at the venue?'

'Oh yes,' I said, remembering the conversation. 'Sorry, bit absent-minded this evening.'

I opened the folder and had a quick look. There at the top was a photo of Sarah and Josh in front of the Sacré-Coeur, looking blissfully happy. 'I look forward to having a look at these. I think they'll be great for telling the story of your relationship, so that everyone gets a glimpse into what makes the two of you, you.'

'I think it's a nice idea. Sarah's been pretty busy, you know how it is this time of year. And now she's gone to Berlin for the weekend with a friend. But I found these in our photo albums.'

'Great.' I put the folder to one side. 'Do you want some hot chocolate? I just made it.'

'Sure,' he said, slipping off his jacket, 'OK if I put this on your radiator? It's wet through with snow.'

I nodded, and got the drink for him. We sat together on the sofa. 'Not long now,' I said. 'Is it all starting to feel real yet?'

'Getting there,' he said, with a smile.

'Your family OK about it all now?'

'They're coming round. I mean it's still upsetting that my grandma won't be able to make it . . . and it's affected a few people on my side of the family –' He glanced down at the floor. 'But we're doing what Sarah wants, and like she says, she's the one I'm marrying. But it's complicated. I guess you make compromises, don't you?'

He sighed, and sat back. 'Amazing hot chocolate, Haze. How come you never made this when we were working together?'

'I don't know. I've rediscovered a few things, since I left work. Baking, cooking, daytime pyjama-wearing . . .'

He smiled. 'Living the dream, eh.'

'I'm lucky enough to like the people I work with too, and that helps.'

'Whereas I'm stuck with all the people you decided you didn't like.' He laughed good-naturedly.

I smiled.

'What are these,' he said, picking up the tickets I'd left out on the coffee table. '*The Nutcracker*? The one your sister's in, right? Nice,' he commented.

'Yes. It's been getting great reviews, Lila's thrilled. I'm looking forward to it.'

He glanced at the date as he put them back down. 'Hey, these are for tonight – am I keeping you?'

'No,' I said, 'Well, yes and no.'

He raised an eyebrow.

'I was supposed to be going with Amber, but she's been busy up at the cake shop, with her mum, magazine shoot – fantastic opportunity and . . .'

'There's one going?' Josh said, his eyes brightening. 'I mean . . . it's horribly presumptuous of me, obviously. I'm sure you've had a better offer. But I've always wanted to go to the Royal Opera House.'

'You're serious?' I said.

I'd lost sight of my moral compass. Josh seemed to think

this was fine. I mean, we had been friends for a while. And just because he was getting married, it didn't mean he couldn't have female friends . . . Or did it?

'Sure,' I said, before I could change my mind. 'Let's go.'

I didn't go for the red dress in the end. Josh persuaded me to keep the jumper, so I switched up to some black jeans and put sheepskin boots on with it. I pulled on my biggest coat, a vintage fake fur that always made me feel like Flossie Teacake. It wasn't what I'd pictured myself going to the ballet in, but the moment we got outside and the icy blast of December snow hit, I was grateful I had followed his advice.

'Sod the bus. It's too cold for standing at a bus stop in this weather.' He flagged down a black cab and we jumped inside.

I sat down on the seat beside him and looked out as the city took on a new, wintry look, a frosting of white gathering on the car roofs and postboxes.

'I've never actually been in a black cab before,' I confessed, turning to him.

'You're kidding,' he smiled. 'Never?'

'Not once. When Lila and I first got here we were scrimping and saving. I kind of prided myself on getting to know the bus routes so well.'

'Not even at work, though?' he asked.

I shook my head. 'Come on, Josh. We both know I was way too junior to be expensing things like that.'

'Well, here we are,' he said, his eyes creasing as he smiled. 'I feel kind of honoured to be sharing it with you.'

We watched the city, the excited rush and bustle of people trying to shelter from the weather, and hurrying home with bags of Christmas shopping. We sat in companionable silence, until the taxi pulled up near to the Royal Opera House.

Josh and I walked up the steps and in through the main entrance, and I felt a wave of nerves.

'You're crossing your fingers,' he said, glancing down at my hand.

I smiled, as I saw he was right. It had been unconscious.

'For Lila?'

'Yes. For Lila.'

I didn't need to, of course. Lila's performance was exquisite – and it wasn't down to silently wishing her luck – it was because she was dedicated and brilliant at what she did. Watching her glide across the stage, I felt a swell of pride. That was my sister up there – the girl I'd grown up with, shared almost every special moment of my life with. And now she was a star.

Lila didn't need my help any more. She didn't need saving. She didn't need anyone's help at all. She was going to be just fine.

I was conscious of Josh's presence beside me. Feeling relaxed, and calm in his company, and delighting in the way he enjoyed the show, and the surroundings. I was glad he'd asked to come. I imagined the empty seat that would have been next to me, and was glad that it was filled by him.

When the show drew to a close, and the performers came to take a bow, Josh and I filed out into the foyer with the rest of the audience. 'Drink?' he said.

'Yes,' I answered. 'But let's have one backstage.' I smiled at him mischievously, and led him around to the stage door.

Lila met us there, like we'd agreed, and led us through into her dressing room. 'I'm so glad you came,' she squealed. 'And who's this?' she asked. Her eyes were bright, intrigued.

'This is Josh,' I said, introducing them. I needed to dispel the misunderstanding right away, because things were starting to feel weird. 'I'm his ... well, we're friends.'

'Hazel's my wedding planner,' Josh said simply.

Lila nodded. He probably didn't notice the subtly raised eyebrow, which I knew was directed at me, Lila's trademark expression of suspicion and/or disbelief.

'Anything to drink back here?' I asked. I realised my error immediately. Surrounded by ballerinas ... it was looking a little unlikely now.

'No,' Lila said, her face breaking into a smile. 'Get me out of here,' she whispered. 'Because that was the last performance of the week for me, and I could really do with one.'

We met Ollie at a pub around the corner, and I ordered in mulled wine for us all.

'So, what did you think of the show?' Ollie asked.

'It was brilliant,' Josh answered. 'I don't know much about ballet, I have to admit, but I thought it was great.'

'I'm with you there,' Ollie said. 'I didn't have a clue about it before I got together with Lila, but she's totally sold me on it. I've already seen her in this one twice, and I must've seen her practising it in our bedroom over a hundred times. I don't think I could get tired of it.'

'Thanks, guys,' Lila said. 'I appreciate the support. I don't know what I'll do when this is all over. With the wedding, then this – this year's all been a bit of a dream, really.'

'Of course, your wedding,' Josh said, 'Hazel mentioned that to me – congratulations.'

'Thanks,' Ollie said. 'Best day of my life. And you're in wonderfully safe hands with Hazel in charge of yours, I promise you that.'

'She's been fantastic. Dealt with more than one drama and kept us both calm, which has probably been the most important thing.'

'Where's the wedding going to be?' Ollie asked.

'Cuba,' Josh said, 'on the beach.'

'Oh fantastic,' Ollie said. 'Great way of escaping all those troublesome family members and friends, eh.'

'Yes.' I still saw it there, the tug of conflicting emotions in Josh's eyes. 'Just a select few there on the day. That's how we wanted it.'

'You'll be the only ones in London with a tan in January,' Lila said. 'Lucky things.'

'You going too, Hazel?' Ollie asked.

I shook my head. 'No. My job will be done by then.'

That evening, Josh walked me home. Amber had texted to say she'd be staying at her parents' house overnight, so the flat was empty.

'Do want to come upstairs for a drink?' I asked.

'Sure,' he said. 'Why not?'

I poured us out a glass of wine each, then excused myself to go to the bathroom.

Once in there, I gave myself a very stern look in the mirror. I would design a brilliant, inspiring wedding for these two, just as if they were any other clients.

I had to keep this friendly, and professional. It probably wasn't my best idea inviting him back in the first place, but now he was here, I had to keep control.

I heard Josh's voice as I emerged from the bathroom: 'Wow.'

I looked towards the living room, but it was empty.

I stepped out into the hallway, and felt a rising sense of panic. I looked into my bedroom, one of the only places he could be. But he wouldn't. *Would he?*

'Sorry,' he said, ducking his head out of my bedroom. 'Crappiest manners ever. Apologies. Your alarm clock started going off and so I ducked in here to switch it off. Didn't mean to snoop around. But Hazel—' he took me by the hand and pulled me into the room. As he did so a shot of electricity bolted through me, and I felt a flush rise to my cheeks.

'These are wonderful, Haze.'

I was confronted by my own sets – the ones I'd carefully constructed over the years, the tiny dolls' houses that Sam had once mocked. I'd left my closet open. The flush in my face heated up until my ears were burning.

'You shouldn't have come in here,' I said. 'This stuff . . . it's not . . . I mean it's stupid. A stupid hobby . . .'

'Don't talk rubbish,' Josh said, turning to me. 'These are beautiful. These are some of the most beautiful things I've ever seen. No wonder you were so good at work, and with weddings – you've been running people's lives the whole time, here.'

I caught his eye, in spite of my slight embarrassment at how spot-on his comment was, and was rewarded by a genuine smile. 'Hazel. These are wonderful. You've got what it takes to make it as a set designer, and you've been hiding your talent away for far too long.'

Josh left at midnight but I wasn't tired. I picked up the folder of photos and started to look through it.

Josh and Sarah at their graduation.

Josh and Sarah with their families at Christmas.

Josh and Sarah on a summer picnic with friends.

Josh and Sarah, just together – their faces pressed together as they took the selfie.

What was I doing?

I was going to finish planning their wedding, profession-ally. Just as if being with Josh– I thought of his smile, and my heart lifted a little. Just as if being with Josh made me feel nothing at all.

Chapter 37

Two days later, Josh and I were at a café in town, the coffees between us completely untouched.

'What do you mean, missing?' I said.

'She was due back from Berlin yesterday, but she never arrived. She hasn't returned any of my calls, and now it seems like her phone's off.'

'Let me try it,' I said. I picked up my mobile and called through to Sarah, but it went straight to answerphone. 'Same thing here. Have you spoken to her family?'

'Yes, I called her mum this morning, but she was typically laidback about the whole thing. She said Sarah's a free bird, and I shouldn't try and keep her caged, something like that.' Josh said, shaking his head.

'Well that's all well and good provided she's not in a ditch somewhere,' I said. I saw the expression on Josh's face and hurriedly tried to take the words back. 'Sorry. I meant . . .

Look, I'm sure she's fine. She's probably just working a few things out in her head right now. She wouldn't be the first bride to need some space.'

'You think she's got cold feet?' Josh said.

'No.' I wondered if it wouldn't be better if I just kept quiet.

'You do, don't you?' Josh bit his lip.

'I have no idea. But obviously you have to find her.'

Josh called round Sarah's friends and family, and I got us some flapjacks as we waited for news.

'No one knows anything,' Josh said. 'But no one seems that worried either – which I suppose is something. I mean this is what she does, Haze. She disappears. I know that – I've always known that.'

I tried to ignore the thought that was nagging at me. Why, if you had Josh, would you ever want to disappear?

Josh went home eventually. The next morning, he called by.

'She's back,' he said, with a smile. 'Sarah. She came back to our house at midnight last night.'

'And she's OK?'

'She's fine. Can I come in?'

'Of course, take a seat,' I got up and had a token attempt at tidying and hurriedly shoved some of the mounting paper-work on my desk to one side.

'So what happened?' I asked.

'She panicked, apparently,' Josh said, running a hand through his dark hair. He had dark circles under his eyes. 'She said she had a picture of herself at the end of the aisle, and suddenly felt it wasn't the right thing after all.'

'What exactly wasn't the right thing, marrying you?' I said, realising I was feeling a little hopeful that the answer might be yes.

'No ... she says it wasn't to do with me. It was getting married full stop. She's got all these ideas about how once she's settled she'll never be able to do all the things she wanted to – go travelling, learn to read tarot cards ...'

'Tarot cards?'

'I know ...' Josh squinted up at me, then rubbed his eyes. 'I didn't even know she was interested in that stuff. You haven't got any coffee, have you?'

'Of course,' I said, getting to my feet and putting the kettle on. 'Sorry. So I'm guessing you didn't get much sleep last night then?'

'Hardly any. We stayed up talking.'

'And?'

'I think we can work things out. I mean, everyone has last-minute nerves, don't they? I've definitely had a few moments of wondering whether we're doing the right thing ... But you work through that, don't you? And I guess that's good preparation for being married – we're going to have a lot of things to work through.'

'Sure,' I said, pouring the coffee and adding milk. I put a mini chocolate Yule log on his saucer and passed it to him.

'I wish I was the right person to give you advice on married life – but I'm afraid I'm not.'

Josh shook his head. 'No one really knows the answer, do they?'

'So where do you two stand now?' I asked.

'We're OK. So that's why I really came by. To tell you everything is back on. Sarah and I are working through this hiccup, and we still want to have the wedding just as before. Thanks for being patient with us.'

'Great,' I said, with a smile. And it was, wasn't it? Josh and Sarah, two of my clients, who loved each other very much, were going to tie the knot on a Caribbean beach, at a wedding they would remember for the rest of their lives. So why was I having to force this smile?

'Great,' Josh said. His brown eyes met mine and it was a while before he looked away.

Chapter 38

A week later, I met with Lila at her local bakery, the Sweet Tree.

'How are Sarah and Josh?'

'Fine, yes. Everything's sorted. It'll be the most fantastic Caribbean wedding ever. We had a bit of a hiccup when Sarah went AWOL, but she's back now.'

'A bit of a hiccup?' Lila said. 'Sounds like more than that. Are you sure everything's OK?'

'Yes. Josh said they've talked everything through and they're surer than ever that this is what they want.'

'Right,' Lila said, unconvinced.

'Although I guess I do wonder,' I said. 'I mean, if she was really that unsure about marrying him –'

Lila looked at me sternly. 'Stop right there,' she said.

'What?' I said, innocently.

'My God, Hazel. You've got a crush on him, haven't you?'

'NO,' I said, aghast. 'No way. I haven't.'

'I thought that was what was going on,' Lila said, shaking her head. 'You actually *want* them to call off the wedding, don't you?'

'Of course not,' I protested. 'I just spent the morning making sure there would be rose petals on their bed in the honeymoon suite, and a private boat to take them out to the island hotel. Why would I do that, if I didn't want them to get married?'

'I don't know. You tell me.'

Back at home, I opened the folder for forthcoming weddings, and there on the top were Josh and Sarah's details. I felt a pull at my heart. I hadn't heard from either of them for a while, so I could only assume that everything was going ahead as normal after Sarah's brief wobble.

It nagged at me – that Lila was right. I missed Josh. I missed talking to him, missed joking with him. It was wrong. I knew that. But that didn't mean it wasn't happening.

I went out to the shops and called Josh's mobile on the way. No answer. He must be busy. He hadn't answered all week. But then . . . a gut feeling kicked in. Josh didn't do this. He always picked up, even if it was just to say he'd call back later.

I tried him one more time, then called Sarah.

Chapter 39

Sarah came and met me at a café between our two flats. Her hair was swept up into a loose topknot, and she looked relaxed.

'It's over,' she said bluntly.

'What?' I gasped.

'Me and Josh. Finito.' She gave a nonchalant little smile.

'Are you serious? What happened?'

'Oh I think it's been coming for a while. We were burying our heads in the sand, both of us. I mean, surely you noticed that we couldn't agree on a thing when it came to the wedding ... hardly the most auspicious start to a life together, is it?'

'I suppose,' I said, hesitantly. 'But lots of couples disagree on the details, it can be a very stressful time ...'

'Come on, Hazel. You know as well as me it wasn't just a case of the details with us.'

'Are you OK?'

'I've never felt better,' she said lightly.

'You just decided, then?'

'Yes. Woke up, looked over at the man on the pillow next to me – and well, you either know you're meant to be together for ever, or you realise your relationship's past its sell-by date. In our case it was the latter. You know – when you booked the wedding for us, all I could think was – this is a perfect holiday . . . but for someone else.'

'Right,' I said, still struggling a little to take it all in.

'Don't worry about the money,' Sarah said, misreading my expression. 'We know we've incurred some costs, and I'm happy to cover them, including your fee. Small price to pay really, if you think that we've just escaped a lifetime with the wrong person.'

Sarah got up to leave. She got as far as the door, then turned around. 'And thanks, Hazel. I know this isn't quite the way things were meant to turn out.'

I glanced across at her empty chair, and the full cup of coffee she'd left. She'd walked out of the café just the way I remember her arriving at our first meeting, in a swirl of coloured fabrics, her feet so light on the floor she could have been floating. The sparkle in her eye told me she was already past the point of no return.

Maybe some people were better on their own. She certainly seemed freer and happier than she had at any point while we'd been planning the wedding.

There was one thing I hadn't asked. Josh was out there somewhere, alone – and quite possibly devastated. I had to find him.

I walked down to the canal, and back through the park. I continued to call Josh on my mobile, even though each time it rang through to voicemail. There was something comforting in hearing his voice, so calm and normal – and I wondered if the mood of that recorded message was even close to how he might be feeling now.

I didn't know what Josh's regular hang-outs were. But this park was where we had sometimes gone for lunch, which was as close to a starting point as I had here in the mist and tangle of the city.

I jumped a little as my phone buzzed with a message.

<SMS>*Haze. I'm on the bandstand. Come over. Josh.*

I looked up and saw a silhouetted figure just metres away. He was there. I picked up my pace and closed the distance between us.

I greeted him with a hug. 'Found you.'

'Sorry I didn't pick up when you called.'

'Don't worry. I understand.' I paused for a moment. 'I spoke to Sarah this morning.'

'Right,' he said, his eyes downcast. 'So you know.'

'Yes.' We sat down together on the concrete of the bandstand, leaning against the intricate steel railings.

'What a mess we've made of everything.'

I looked him in the eye. 'I'm sorry. It must be hard.'

'I wanted to do the right thing, Haze. But this is where it led to. Us breaking up.'

There was a sadness in his eyes that made me want to reach out and touch him.

'How are you feeling?'

'Honestly? Like I've let everyone down. My family . . . God, I've no idea how I'm going to tell them. Then our friends, the guests who've already booked flights . . .'

'I can help to sort some of that out,' I said.

'No.' he shook his head. 'This is our mess to clear up now. We've already dragged you into enough of this.'

'People will understand,' I said. 'Or at least they will in time.'

He looked at me again and let out a sigh. 'I guess.'

'Anyway, that wasn't really what I meant. I was asking how you're feeling. About what happened, about breaking up with Sarah.'

He paused. 'This seems like an awful thing to say.'

'Go on.'

'But I think I feel OK. More than that. I'm pretty sure I feel relieved.'

Chapter 40

On Friday evening I went around to Lila's, and we baked together using Grandma Joyce's recipe for Christmas biscuits; we always ate those in the final days of Advent. It was the only time Lila baked, and I treasured these moments together. Tonight it was just what I needed, the time and space away from the drama of Josh and Sarah's break-up, and the fact that out of three weddings on my books one had dissolved right in front of my eyes.

'How are things coming along with Eliot and Gemma's wedding?' Lila asked, as she pressed out Christmas tree shapes with a biscuit cutter.

'Better than they were. Eliot and Gemma are pretty much all set, I called the venue this morning to make the final arrangements, and I've found a great caller for the Ceilidh. Glad I won't have to spell that in an email ever again.' I smiled.

'Well, we're really excited about it. I bought my dress the other day, and we've booked the train up. It's miles!'

'I know – but it will be worth it, I promise.'

'I can't wait. It's such a relief to know there are only a couple of performances left, and then it's time to relax and party.'

'You deserve it. What an amazing show.'

'You know, I was thinking something,' Lila said, pausing with the cookie cutter held aloft. 'You should talk to the art director. He's really nice.'

'Me. Don't be silly,' I said, feeling my face flush.

'I'm serious,' Lila said. 'The designer they worked with this time had great vision but was really unreliable. Xander, the art director, was talking about trying someone new, or pairing the designer up with someone for the shows in the new year. We get on well and I couldn't resist talking about how talented you are. He's interested in meeting you. If you'd like to, that is?'

'Erm, yes,' I said, struggling to believe this was really happening.

'No guarantees, but it's worth a try, surely?' Lila said, with a smile.

'Definitely,' I said, sounding surer than I felt. I thought of the sets in my cupboard, and my portfolio of work – neither of which I'd shared in a professional sense for years. The thought of showing them to someone at the Royal Opera

House was surreal and terrifying. But when I thought of Josh's encouraging words when he'd seen my work, it all, at somehow, felt possible.

'So back to Bidcombe we go this Christmas,' Lila said, jolting me out of my thoughts.

'Yes. Back to the cottage.'

'How do you think Ben's getting on there?' Lila enquired.

'He seems well,' I said. 'No job yet, so I guess there's always the risk he could end up staying there for ever . . .'

'Like Sam?'

'God, yes.' I felt a pang of guilt saying it. Sam was still my friend, after all, even if we weren't really talking to each other at the moment. 'I suppose so. But I don't think he'll stick around that long. You know how ambitious Ben's always been. I think he's just having a bit of downtime.'

'Ollie's looking forward to it,' Lila said. 'With the requisite dose of trepidation.'

'His first Delaney Christmas, poor guy,' I laughed. 'Well, part of the deal now that you guys are married, I guess. I'll go easy on him. Can't promise the same for Mum and Dad, though.'

After talking with Lila, I'd sent Xander at the Royal Opera House an email and he'd replied immediately suggesting I come in for an informal meeting. I could barely sleep that night thinking about it. As the sky brightened outside, I took out one of my sets from the cupboard – a model for Swan Lake that I'd made, just for pleasure, while Lila had been performing it a couple of years back. I decided to take it with me today, along with my portfolio.

I got a taxi over to Covent Garden, remembering the journey with Josh, and walked beneath the twinkling Christmas lights in Wellington Street, clutching the set tightly. I was nervous, but I was ready.

I came out of the side entrance an hour later. A light snow had dusted the pavements and taxi roofs. I waited less than a second before getting out my mobile and calling Lila.

'Good news,' I said, when she picked up. 'He's going to give me a chance. Starting on a project in January.'

Lila's squeal was so loud I held the phone away from my ear, and laughed.

'Congratulations,' she said.

'I can't really believe it.'

'Believe it!' Lila said.

And as I walked through the cobbled piazza, carol singers singing and children running excitedly in and out of the toy shops, I started to.

Back at home, I put the set back in my cupboard. I thought of Josh – it had been the one he'd liked most. I thought of his warm smile when he'd been here and seen my sets for the first time. Now that we no longer worked together, I'd have no reason to see him at all. The thought made me feel desperately sad. Josh was the man who made me smile, made me laugh, made me feel best about being me.

Maybe Lila was right. Maybe I was scared of really feeling something.

I dialled Josh's number, and as he picked up I almost lost my nerve. I gathered my strength and asked him.

'Have you ever been to Scotland?'

'No,' he said curious. 'But I've always wanted to.'

'Excellent.'

This was insane. But I'd come this far.

'Because you're coming with me, next weekend.'

Chapter 41

19 December

Castle Belvedere, Scotland

I looked out of the kitchen window. People scurried through the park, dressed warmly in coats and scarves, and laden with shopping bags. The window panes were lacy with frost. 'It looks freezing out there,' I said. 'Which bodes well, I hope.'

Amber and I were in the kitchen with her mum Ella, putting the final touches to Eliot and Gemma's wedding cake. It looked spectacular – red roses dotted around the edges, and silver balls adding a little sparkle.

'How's the forecast for tomorrow looking?'

I'd been clicking on the Met Office app on my phone for days now, with the Scottish region where Castle Belvedere was set as my default location, but the forecast kept changing.

'Varying hour to hour at the moment,' I said. 'I guess we'll just have to wait and see.'

'Lucky we've got a four-wheel drive, then,' Ella said warmly. It felt natural to have her here in our kitchen, some-how. She was the honey-coloured warm to pale, dark-haired Amber's cool. She and Amber worked together seamlessly, mixing and icing, chatting as they went. After her initial reservations about working with her mum, Amber had come around to the idea – she had decided to set up a company that would be an off-shoot from her mum's shop. So they both worked independently, but for the same business.

'It's going to be quite an adventure getting this cake up there,' Amber added.

'Thanks for driving,' I replied. 'Above and beyond the call of duty, really.'

'Oh there's no such thing,' Ella assured me. 'With Amber building up the wedding arm of the business we need to get word of mouth spreading.'

'And even if that weren't the case,' Amber said. 'I don't think we'd trust anyone else to get this baby up there in one piece, quite frankly.'

'You all set?' Ella said.

I flicked through the train tickets in my wallet – one for me, going up today, the day before the wedding, and return-ing the day after, and one for Josh, who'd be arriving tomorrow morning.

'Yes, I think so.' I glanced down at my bag, ran through in my mind the things I'd put in there – most of it on the iPad, but print-outs of the schedule and final to-do lists. I would be arriving at the castle tonight, helping to settle the guests and attend to the welcome meal at a nearby restaurant.

I felt a flicker of excitement at the prospect of Josh meeting me there, but it was tempered with uncertainty. Had I been too hasty in inviting him? Sarah had only just disappeared from view, after all, and while he seemed calm and accepting of what had happened, there was every chance that shock was masking his grief, and that reality would set in once we were away. But – I told myself – a change of scene and the chance to meet some new people would do him good. Plus I wanted him there. I really wanted him there.

'Do you think it's pumping the right amount of snow?' I asked Josh, the next day. 'I mean, this is a bit of a blizzard – I think Gemma had more of a picturesque light dusting in mind.'

The snow machine I had arranged at the eleventh hour was positioned behind a bush next to the entrance of Belvedere Castle, and was hurling out fake snow. If I got the angle right, it would mean that when the bride arrived, she would have snowflakes under foot as she approached the castle, just as we had discussed – but just a few degrees out and Gemma would be saying her vows with clumps of white in her hair.

'Surely she's not going to care once she's here,' Josh said, checking the side of the machine for instructions. 'She'll be so caught up in the moment.'

I furrowed my brow. 'You haven't met Gemma.'

'Ah, right. I see.'

It was true that Gemma had softened in her approach over the last couple of weeks, though. Coming so close to everything falling apart seemed to have nudged her into letting go of some of the smaller details on the wedding. She was no longer fretting over the wedding favours – but it certainly wasn't safe to assume that she wouldn't mind if the bigger things went wrong.

I checked my phone. 'I can leave you to sort this, can't I, Josh? It's just the hairdresser and make-up artist are due to arrive, and I need to direct them to the room where me and her bridesmaids are staying.'

He looked bemused. 'I thought I was supposed to be a guest here?'

'Not just any guest. You're my plus one,' I smiled. 'And that means you have to muck in a bit.'

'And there was I thinking that with my own wedding getting cancelled, I'd be off the hook.'

'No way,' I smiled.

I squinted through the mist of hairspray, and arranged the bouquets on the bride's bedspread.

'So, bridesmaids, here are spreadsheets for the day. Everything's on there for you.'

Tess, Gemma's six-year-old niece and flowergirl, was toying with the satin ribbon on her dress. 'And you, sweetheart. Are you still OK to sprinkle the rose petals and glass pebbles on the table?'

Tess nodded. 'I'm excited.'

She looked over at Gemma, who was sitting in front of the mirror with large heated rollers in her hair, her hairdresser tonging loose strands at the front into ringlets. She motioned for me to bend to her level.

'Auntie Gemma looks funny,' she whispered in my ear. 'I think she looks prettier without those things.'

I let out a laugh. I rearranged a small pink rosebud that had come loose from Tess's hairband. 'Don't worry, they aren't staying in. Your auntie's going to look better in a minute.'

'Are you sure this is going to look all right?' Gemma said, putting her hand up to the front of her hair. 'You don't think it's getting a bit too, you know, ringletty? I don't want to look like Annie.'

I got the feeling it was time to top up the bubbles. I opened the window and picked up the bottle of Champagne from the window ledge, where it was staying cool. 'Top up, anyone?' I offered the bottle to Gemma. She looked relieved, and held out her glass.

'You don't think ringlets are a bit . . .? I don't know . . .' she pulled one straight in the mirror. Gemma took a deep breath, then glanced over at me, a look of desperation in her eyes. 'Done?'

'They're classic,' I said.

'Do I want classic, though?' Gemma twisted her mouth to the side.

I bit my tongue. Classic and traditional had been Gemma's keywords from day one.

'I want something people will remember. Something – unique. I can't go in looking like this. The more I look at it, the more I feel just like every other bride.'

'I've got an idea,' I said. 'I'll be right back.'

I dashed downstairs and out of the front door, and was hit by a blast of snowflakes. I put my hands out in front of me and blocked it. I caught sight of Josh hammering at the side of the machine. 'How do you stop this thing?'

I found the button and we both started to laugh. 'I don't think that's quite the effect Eliot and Gemma had in mind . . .' I said.

'It's like a power hose,' Josh said. 'Enough to send Gemma flying.'

'I'll take a look at the settings. In the meantime, Josh – could you do me a favour? Collect some mistletoe? We need enough to make a tiara with.'

'Your wish – or should I say Gemma's wish – is my command,' Josh said. Before he left he looked back at me struggling with the snow machine. 'Good luck with that thing.' Somehow, with his warm gaze on me, it didn't seem so bad.

'Ha!' I said, finding a button on the underside of the machine and pressing it. It sent out a gentler spray of fake snow, then juddered to a complete stop.

I pressed the other buttons, trying to restart the machine. 'Hazel!' came the call from Gemma's room. 'My hair!' With increasing desperation, I punched at the buttons, but nothing would persuade the machine to restart.

I checked my phone. We were at wedding minus one hour – and I had promised Gemma and Eliot a white winter wedding.

'Hazel!' Josh, metres away across the lawn, had turned around to face me, and was pointing directly in front of him. 'Look!'

I squinted, trying to make out what he was pointing at. I couldn't see a thing.

'There,' he said, pointing again.

Then I saw it – falling gently, dots of white against the green backdrop of the highlands, were the tiniest flakes of snow.

I checked my watch. It was only half an hour before the ceremony, and while guests had started pouring into the venue, Amber and Ella – and, most importantly, the cake – were nowhere to be seen. I smiled and greeted the guests one by one, leading them through to a warm lounge where there was space to relax ahead of the ceremony.

As Eliot and Gemma's friends and family mingled, and a buzz built up in the lounge, I escaped to a quiet hotel bedroom to call Amber.

'Where are you?' I whispered urgently when she picked up.

'We're on our way. Don't worry.'

'Don't worry? How can I not worry?' I hissed back. 'It's midday and you're not here. Please at least tell me you and your mum haven't disappeared down a crevasse somewhere.'

I heard Ella's voice shouting out. 'We're fine, Hazel. Tell her we're fine, Amber.'

'We're fine,' Amber said. 'And no, we're not in a crevasse. We're just stuck behind some rather stubborn sheep at the moment, that's all.'

'Sheep?' I said, no longer able to disguise my building panic. 'These two are about to get married, and we're one wedding cake and a village of gingerbread houses short of a reception right now.'

'Cool your boots,' Amber said. 'We'll be there. Chill.'

I put down the phone, hoping with every bone in my body that they would be right.

Lila and Ollie came in to the lounge, and after greeting their friends, came over to me. Lila looked beautiful in a knee-length green silk dress, and a fur stole, her blonde hair swept up and to the side, pinned with a clip made from holly berries.

'You look great,' I said. She smiled. 'Well, we made it, which is the main thing. You guys didn't pick the easiest venue in the world to find.'

'Part of what makes it so special,' I said. I was still quietly praying that it wouldn't be so special that it proved impossible for Amber and Ella to find. 'You settled in to your room OK?'

'Yes – it's fantastic,' Ollie said. 'View out across the forest. It's so peaceful round here, isn't it, Lila?'

'A lovely change from the city,' Lila said. 'Just what we both needed.'

It was heartening to see my sister looking so relaxed.

'Listen, I'd love to stay and chat, but I'd better make sure everything's in order.' With a flood of relied, I spotted Amber and her mum coming in with the cake.

'Sure,' Lila said. 'We know you're on duty today, don't worry. Let's chat later this evening.'

She kissed me on my cheek and we hugged. It was her cheek pressed against mine this time, gently but firmly as if she didn't really want us to part. Something had changed. But I didn't know what.

Gemma and Eliot's entrance hadn't exactly been usual. He'd rented a private plane for the day, and with the crowds gathered round to watch, he'd brought his beautiful bride in to land in the grounds close to the castle. Gemma had hauled out her full dress and they'd walked arm in arm up to the venue to hoots and cheers, a flurry of snowflakes falling around them.

Now, here we all were, in a grand room at Castle Belvedere, watching them about to get married. Josh was standing next to me.

'Will you take this woman,' the celebrant said, 'to be your lawfully wedded wife?'

'I will,' Eliot said. Standing at the top of the aisle, a red rose in the lapel of his suit, he looked strikingly handsome. I could hear the quiver in his voice as he spoke, holding his bride's hand in his.

Gemma, in her floor-length ivory dress with lace bolero, and a twisted mistletoe tiara in her hair, seemed completely content and at peace as she stood with her groom.

Now, emotion was all well and good. But there was no way I was going to relax until they'd said their vows.

'Will you take this man,' he continued, 'to be your . . .'

'YES,' Gemma squealed.

'I have to finish,' the man said, laughing. 'Your lawfully wedded husband?'

'Yes, yes, YES,' she squealed again. She kissed Eliot on his mouth, hard, and the crowd let out a cheer.

It was DONE. I smiled with relief. Months in the planning, a dozen or more sleepless nights along the way, a budget that had been broken more than once, and Gemma and Eliot were finally man and wife. And they'd had a proper dusting of real snow, after all.

Instinctively, I took Josh's hand and squeezed it gently. He turned to look at me, and I felt a tingle that started in the pit of my stomach and spread right down to my toes.

The caller at the Ceilidh boomed out a new command: 'All spin with new partners.' Before I'd heard the end of the sentence, Eliot's father, a broad-shouldered man in a kilt, had swept me round in a circle and by the end of the dance I was bent double with laughter and gasping for breath.

'Well, that was an experience,' I said breathlessly, as I caught up with Josh back at our table.

'You're a natural,' Josh said.

'You were watching?'

'Of course I was watching,' he said. His cheeks coloured in a way that you could have missed, but I didn't.

'And it was only right that they let you go off duty.'

'I still can't believe it's all worked out. They really did it.'

'They?'

Josh raised an eyebrow.

'OK. WE really did it.'

Lila and I found a quiet moment to talk to each other.

'I have a feeling this is going to be a good year,' I said.

'Are you going to keep going with the weddings?' she asked.

I shook my head, and felt sure about what I really wanted. 'It's a brilliant job – for someone else. Not for me. I'm done with fixing everyone else's lives – I'm going to focus on my own for a while.'

'Well, for what it's worth, I think you're doing the right thing,' Lila said.

A smile spread across Lila's face, and I felt mine mirror it. 'Hopefully one day soon I'll be dancing in one of your sets.'

'I hope so,' I said, picturing it and smiling.

'I've got some good news too,' Lila said, biting her lip.

'Oh yes?'

'It turns out that my worries were a little unfounded.'

I raised a questioning eyebrow.

'I'm pregnant, Hazel. You're going to be an auntie.'

It took a moment for her words to sink in. The most incredible, happy news I could have hoped to hear.

'Just seven weeks. But I couldn't wait to tell you.'

Tears prickled at my eyes and I realised that this meant more to me, more than anything else – more than the weddings, more than my career. Far more than that. That my twin sister was happy.

I put my arms around her and drew her towards me and into a hug. There, as her soft blonde hair brushed gently against my cheek and her arms were looped around my waist, I realised I wasn't holding her up any longer. It was as if her light ballerina feet were rooted more firmly in the earth than they ever had been before.

'Come outside with me,' Josh said, later that evening. 'There's something I wanted to show you.'

He took me by the hand and led me out through a side door in the castle, to a terrace overlooking the manicured gardens and the mountains beyond. There was frost on the ground and the air was chilly. I shivered. Josh took off his suit jacket and handed it to me.

'Thanks.'

'You're welcome. Look up,' he said.

I tilted my head back and my high heels wobbled on the gravel. Josh steadied me.

The sky was bright with stars, white light that shone down on us in minuscule beams.

'Isn't it beautiful?' Josh said.

'Yes.' I wanted to enjoy it, this moment. But one thing nagged at me. 'Josh, do you still think about Sarah?'

Josh paused. 'Of course I do. And I'll never regret being with her. She's a very special person.'

A heavy feeling settled in my heart. 'Yes, she is,' I said, feeling deflated. 'So you two are in touch again?'

'No,' Josh said, wrinkling his brow. 'I mean, I'm sure we will be, but for now I think a clean break is probably best for both of us. I suppose we needed to get engaged in order to know for sure – somehow we just needed to see it through.'

'Right. And you're OK with how things turned out?'

'Almost OK,' he smiled. 'I'm hoping they might still be turning out.'

'What do you mean?'

'Come on, Hazel. You must have guessed. The way I always found an excuse to work with you – the fact that I'm up here, freezing at a wedding with you right now and spent the morning collecting mistletoe in the woods.'

I stood and listened, feeling suddenly shy.

'I wanted to be with you,' he said. 'I *want* to be with you.'

'Oh.'

I looked down at our hands, ran a thumb over the skin on the back of Josh's. Even outside, it was warm to the touch. I looked up at his face, those warm brown eyes, his full lips.

'Oh?' he echoed, smiling.

I put a finger on his lips and then replaced it with my mouth, our lips meeting in a featherlight kiss that sent a shiver through me. 'I'm not always great with words. I want to be with you too.'

'Good,' Josh said, putting his arms around me and bringing me close. 'I was really, really hoping you would say that.' I relished the warmth of his body against mine, the security of his arms around me. Through the window, we could hear the strains of the Ceilidh, music, laughter ... but out on the roof terrace we were a world away from it all.

Chapter 42

24 December

Christmas at the Delaney house

In the family cottage back in Bidcombe on Christmas Eve, Lila, Ollie, me, Ben and Mum and Dad were sitting around the fire on armchairs and on the rug, eating mince pies and listening to carols. If you were to glance in through the window, you would think our family was always like this – calm, harmonious, delighting in each other's company, not a worry in the world. But the year had tested each of us, and to be here together now, well the moment was all the more precious for that. Ben filled up Mum and Dad's glasses, and Ollie whispered something to Lila, touching her fleetingly on her stomach, a reminder of all that next year had in store. I sank back into the armchair, happy this time to keep quiet, just to watch the people I loved most as they talked to one another. The next day would be a whirlwind, I knew – with Grandma Joyce and her friend Rosie arriving, visits from the neighbours and a flurry of activity in the kitchen before the cracker-pulling started – but tonight was calm.

It's easy to think, isn't it, that Christmas is all about the glitter and baubles – the chocolate Advent calendars and the silver ribbons wrapped around perfectly chosen presents. And it is. Part of it is about that.

But it's also about the imperfections. The presents that aren't quite right, the bad jokes, the flushed cheeks and wonky Christmas hats.

I catch Lila looking at Ollie and see the love in her eyes. She is separate from me, but my other half as much as ever. And she's strong again. Lila – who didn't get dragged back down, after all. It will always be there, on the seabed of Lila's soul. Ready to reach up. But she's ready to swim hard away from it. She doesn't really need us, standing by with our lifeboat, any longer.

My phone buzzed on the coffee table.

'You're getting a lot of texts,' Lila said, the flicker of a smile on her lips. Ben looked over at me, his curiosity ignited.

'Am I?' I said, a little too quickly.

'That thing's barely stopped beeping since you arrived.'

'Ooh, who is it?' Mum said, leaning forward in her chair. She reached towards the coffee table and picked up the phone.

'MUM!' I protested. I reached out to snatch it back, but Lila used her long legs to block me.

'Now look what you've done,' I said, turning to my sister. 'You've unleashed the nosy beast.'

'Mum,' Ben said, trying to take the phone off her. 'Leave Hazel ...'

'JOSH,' Mum said, raising her eyebrows in interest.

'Just a friend,' I said.

'Simon, has Hazel ever mentioned a Josh to you?'

'What was that, love?' Dad said, dozily. 'I'd love another sherry, yes.'

'Josh, Josh?' Lila said. 'I knew it! I just knew it.'

Mum turned to Lila.

'It's a bit complicated,' Lila explained. 'Although I guess he is back on the market now, right, Haze?'

'GIVE ME THAT,' I insisted, forcing my sister's legs off me and getting to my feet, grabbing the phone back.

'Honestly, I'm always the last to know these days,' Mum said. 'I remember the time when you girls used to tell me everything, and now ...'

'What does a woman have to do for a sliver of privacy round here?' I said.

'Divorce us?' Ben volunteered playfully.

I left the living room and sat down on the hallway stairs, four up, the familiar spot where my long phone conversations as a teenager had almost worn the carpet thin.

The Winter Wedding

In the calm of the hallway, I checked the message from Josh.

Hope you're having a good Christmas eve, H. Wish I could be there with you. I am busy getting thrashed at Monopoly here. See you on boxing day. xx

A tingle ran up my spine as I read Josh's words. Christmas felt very different this year.

Epilogue

New Year's Eve

Christmas at our family house had been as lovely, and manic, as I'd expected, and when I arrived back to the relative calm of the flat just before New Year's Eve I had started to miss them all a little. Before that feeling could settle though, Josh arrived.

By my front door there were two suitcases – my own brown leather one, a hand-me-down from my grandmother, and Josh's black one.

'Right, last chance. We definitely want suitcases,' I said to Josh said. 'Are you sure?'

'No. I've changed my mind.'

We'd been mulling over it for days, ever since we'd decided to use Josh and Sarah's honeymoon tickets to go away, just the two of us.

The flights were to Havana, and the deal they'd booked for their honeymoon was at one of the most glamorous all-inclusive resorts on the island. I should know – I'd booked it.

'OK. Right, that's it. Let's switch.'

We went together into the living room, and picked up the rucksacks we'd left lying on the living room floor.

'So this means . . .' Josh said.

'Yes. Forget the posh resort. Let's fly by the seats of our pants,' I said, a smile creeping onto my face.

Stunning as the resort looked in all the photos, I knew that something would nag at me if we went there – how could I stay there in the honeymoon suite, with Josh, and not think of Sarah? I'd booked everything there with the two of them in mind.

'We'll be able to find somewhere to stay out there,' I said. 'We can explore more this way.'

A postcard fluttered through my letterbox and on to the mat.

On the front was a picture of a cow painted in vibrant blues and reds. Intrigued, I flipped it over and read the message.

'It's for both of us,' I said, holding it out so that Josh could read it with me.

To Josh and Hazel. Having a ball here in Goa. Beach parties, glow sticks, face paint, it's like being eighteen all over again. Not sure I really grew up past that, anyway. Thanks for being so cool about everything, Josh. Have a brilliant non-honeymoon. You two are made for each other. Sarah x

'Weird?' I said.

'Strangely, no.' Josh replied.

'Good.'

Josh put his arms around me and pulled me in towards him for a kiss. As I felt his lips on mine, excitement traced a path up my spine and then spilled down my arms in tiny shivers.

Josh was my present and my future. I wasn't looking behind me any more. With Josh by my side, I was ready to look forward.

Acknowledgements

Thank you to Jo Dickinson, my editor – your support, enthusiasm and ideas keep me focused, and somehow you always seem to understand what it was I was really trying to say! To my agent, Caroline Hardman, who is everything a good agent should be, and a lot more.

To the team at Simon & Schuster, thanks for publishing my books beautifully, spreading the word far and wide, and making me feel so at home. To Sara-Jade Virtue, Hayley McMullan, Carla Josephson, Elinor Fewster and Matt Johnson.

Thank you to my readers – you are the best! It is always a joy to hear from you.

Finally, thank you to my family, who all help me to write, and who, when I type The End, are the best people in the world to come back to.